Joseph

1861—A Rumble of War

★ AMERICAN ADVENTURES ★

Joseph
1861—A Rumble of War

Bonnie Pryor

★

Illustrated by Bert Dodson

AN AVON CAMELOT BOOK

AVON BOOKS, INC.
1350 Avenue of the Americas
New York, New York 10019

Contents

ONE

—◆—

Mud Slide

The moment Joseph put his foot on the steep riverbank, he knew he'd made a mistake. Although the sun was shining, it had rained for the last three days. The rains had been heavy, a deluge that caused the river to overflow its banks and flood the town and left the bank a slippery mass of thick mud. Below him the usually shallow river churned with debris from the recent flood. Brush, logs, and even an old rocking chair went rushing past.

A smooth piece of driftwood caught his eye just a few feet below. It would be perfect for mounting the eagle he had just finished carving. Something like that would be sure to win first prize at the fair next summer. Joseph took a step and felt the mud slide under his feet. Suddenly he was sliding helplessly toward the swirling water. Then his fall was stopped short when one of his feet sank into the mud over his ankle. Landing with his head toward the raging river, he struggled and finally managed to pull himself up to a sitting position.

His new school coat was splattered with thick, gooey mud. His stepfather was going to be angry. He wished he had listened to that sensible part of himself that had wanted to go straight home after school. That very morning his stepfather had warned him to stay away from the river. But he'd let his curiosity get the best of him. Now here he was, stuck, and with his clothes ruined.

Joseph struggled to free his foot and turn himself into position to climb back up the bank. A small sapling clung to the slope only a few feet away. He grabbed at it, hoping it would be strong enough to help him pull himself up. But it was just out of reach and his fingers closed on thin air. His struggles had served only to bury his other arm, nearly to the elbow.

He forced himself to sit quietly while he thought of what to do. Although the main street of Branson Mills crossed the river on a sturdy stone bridge, it was several hundred yards away and around a bend. There was no chance anyone would hear his cries. At any rate, most people would be busy cleaning up the dirt and debris from the floodwaters that had swept through the town. In his stepfather's window sash and door factory, the water had been more than two feet deep. The waters had come up so fast there had been no time to save any of the wood.

"Soaked through," he had told Joseph's mother at dinner the night before. "Even the new shipment of lumber. It will warp when it dries," he added with a worried frown.

Joseph had listened to his stepfather's news with interest, but not sympathy. Mr. Byers had married his mother just a month before. After his father died, his mother had been forced to rent two rooms above the millinery shop, and the wages she earned as a seamstress barely fed them. Mr. Byers had met Joseph's mother when he hired her to sew a dress as a gift for his sister who lived in New York. Two months later they had married. Now

Joseph lived in a nice house on High Street. He knew he should be grateful. Still, he could not bring himself to like Mr. Byers, a tall, stern-appearing man much older than Joseph's real father.

Joseph tried again to climb the bank, but the mud beneath him slid some more and he found himself even closer to the water. By now there wasn't an inch of him that wasn't covered with mud. He suspected his situation would look pretty funny if not for the danger.

As if giving voice to that thought, he heard hooting laughter from somewhere above him. "You've got yourself in quite a fix," said a voice. Zachary Young's face appeared at the top of the bank, a mocking grin stretching from ear to ear.

Joseph groaned. Zachary Young was the last person you would want to see if you needed help. Although he was a year older than Joseph, he had missed so much school that he was only in the third grade.

Still grinning, Zachary squatted down and appeared to study Joseph's predicament.

"Can you help me?" Joseph asked.

Zachary nodded. "I can. Problem is, Do I want to? Your new stepdaddy is one of those abolitionists, I heard. There're a lot of people in town who are pretty angry with him. My pa, for one. He says I'm to stay away from your kind."

An angry reply boiled in Joseph's mouth, but Zachary waved his hand. "Don't worry," he said. "I seldom do what my pa says."

Joseph felt the mud moving beneath him. "Hurry. The bank is slipping," he yelled.

The grin faded, and Zachary stood up. "Try to keep still. I'll go get a rope."

While he waited, Joseph tried to keep his mind off the raging river. He thought about what Zachary had said. He didn't care what Zachary thought about him. But what if the other boys in school had been forbidden to be friends with him too? It was hard enough to make friends in a new school without having a new stepfather making everyone in town upset. It was especially unfair because he didn't even agree with Mr. Byers. His real pa had had two slaves to help with the work on the farm. But the day after he had died, they had run away. His mother couldn't afford to hire anyone to track them down. With no help, they had lost the crops and his mother hadn't had enough money to pay the mortgage. The bank had taken the farm, and they had been forced to move to town.

"No," Joseph said to himself, "I don't have much sympathy for slaves."

Mr. Byers didn't believe in keeping slaves, but until those Yankee abolitionists had come to town, he'd kept his feelings quiet. Now he talked to anyone who would listen. He had even written a letter to the newspaper, saying people shouldn't call themselves Christian if they kept slaves.

That really made Joseph bristle. Mr. Byers had no right to talk like that. Half the people in town had slaves. Why, the minister had spoken about the issue in church last Sunday. He'd said there were even slaves in the Bible. He'd said slavery was a good thing because the slaves could learn about Christianity. Everyone had looked at Joseph's stepfather when he said that. But Mr. Byers had stood up right there in church and said, "True Christians don't sell other Christians' children," and walked out.

Mrs. Byers and her sons had stayed to the end

of the service. Her face was red with embarrassment. Afterward everyone had stood around outside talking, but when Mrs. Byers and the boys came out, people looked uncomfortable and no one spoke.

Joseph's thoughts were interrupted by a strange sucking noise off to one side, and he watched in horror as a huge chunk of the bank broke off and slid down into the water. It left a deep dark gash in the bank. Joseph stared, trying to make sense of what he was seeing. The falling mud had revealed a large crack, nearly as tall as a man. Then he suddenly understood. He was looking at the opening to a cave. It had been there all along, hidden under layers of dirt. How often he had climbed this bank without knowing it was there.

"Grab on," Zachary shouted from above him. At the same time Joseph felt the slap of a thick hemp rope. "I'll tie my end around a tree."

Joseph sighed with relief and gratefully wiggled the rope around himself, tying it under his arms. The movement was enough to start that part of the bank sliding again, and in terror Joseph saw another great chunk come crashing down. He heard

Zachary's shout, but it was too late, because his body was encased in suffocating darkness and tumbling out of control. Then he was free of the mud in a shock of wet that told him he was in the water. As his body was tossed about in the swift river, his chest burned with the need for air.

TWO

Rescue

The air he'd been holding burst from him in a shower of bubbles, and Joseph realized he was going to die. Nevertheless, he fought to follow the trail of bubbles. There were sparkles of light flashing behind his eyes. He pictured the water pouring in, filling his lungs as the river claimed his life.

Then, just as he sensed that he was losing consciousness, he was suddenly jerked by the rope still tied under his arms, and his body seemed to fly through the rushing water. There was the cool breath of air on his face as he was yanked to the surface. He gasped with relief, gulping lungfuls of air, while he felt himself being towed swiftly toward the bank. A log rushed by, narrowly missing him and reminding him that he was still in danger.

The slide had left a huge pile of mud at the edge of the river. Even if he managed to climb over it, there was still the slippery bank.

The same thought must have occurred to Zachary. "I'm going to loosen the rope and tow you down a few feet to a spot where you can climb up," he shouted.

Joseph was too weak to do anything but nod to show he understood. He allowed the rope to guide him along the edge of the water. At last he came to a place where the bank was not so steep and was held in place by a few scrubby trees and brush. It was muddy here, too. Still, there were enough grass and weeds to hold the bank in place. Although he was shivering, Joseph scrambled up quickly. He collapsed at the top, still gasping for air.

Zachary's worried face peered down at him. "Are you all right?"

"Y-you saved my life," Joseph stammered as he untied the rope from around his chest.

Zachary's grin was even wider than before. "I

did, didn't I? I thought you were gone for sure for a minute. I got the rope around a tree, but it wasn't tied when all that mud started sliding." He peered over the edge of the bank toward the cave-in. "What a mess!"

Joseph's teeth were chattering so hard they made a clicking noise.

A look of concern wiped out Zachary's smile. "You'd better get on home before you catch your death. Want me to walk with you?"

"I can make it," Joseph said.

"Run, then," Zachary urged him. "It will make you feel warmer." He picked up the rope and began coiling it around his arm.

But Joseph hesitated. "Thank you," he said at last.

Zachary took Joseph's hand and shook it solemnly. Then he looked at his hand. "Yeech! you need a bath."

Joseph's whole body was racked with deep shudders, and he knew the truth of Zachary's warning. He had to get warm and dry. With a wave he turned and raced away. By the time he reached home, he was shaking so hard he couldn't speak.

His little brother, Jared, was sitting on the floor by the big iron cookstove, playing with the toy wagon Joseph had carved for him. Jared had a weak heart, the doctors said, and the sight of Joseph as he burst through the door made his normally pale face look even whiter.

"Mama, something happened to Joseph," he cried.

Joseph's mother came running from the dining room, where she had been putting a fresh cloth on the table. Her skirts were so wide she had to push them through the door. She took one look at Joseph's white face and dripping clothes and ran for some dry towels. "Take off those wet clothes," she said before she left the room.

A few minutes later Joseph was dressed in dry clothes and sitting by the stove with a blanket wrapped around his shoulders. His mother handed him a cup of coffee and watched while he drank it.

Save for the terse command to take off his wet clothing, Joseph's mother had not spoken since he'd arrived home. She was a tiny, nervous woman. Joseph often thought she was like a little bird, singing as she flitted about the house, making sure everything was perfect. There was nothing timid about her stern look tonight as she collapsed into a chair. "I would like an explanation, young man," she said.

Reluctantly Joseph told her everything that had happened. He tried to make it sound less frightening than it really was. Jared listened, too, his eyes wide.

In the middle of the story Mr. Byers arrived home for dinner, and Joseph had to repeat it.

"Didn't I warn you to stay away from the river just this morning?" Mr. Byers asked.

Joseph nodded. "Yes, sir. I just wanted to take a quick look."

"While you're in my house, I expect you to obey," Mr. Byers said curtly. "You may spend the evening in your room thinking about it. There will be no supper."

Joseph avoided looking at his mother's unhappy face. Without a word he stalked to his room. There he threw himself onto his bed and stared at the ceiling. His room was directly over the dining room. From below he could hear the clink of dishes and the steady drone of his stepfather's voice and his mother's occasional murmured reply. He did not hear his brothers' voices, but that did not surprise him. Dinners at home with his real father had been comfortable, a time for laughter and conversation that included everyone in the family. Mr. Byers, however, was like most adults, who believed that children should be seen but not heard at the table. The only words they were allowed to say were "please" and "thank you." Thinking about his father, Joseph closed his eyes.

After a time the conversation ended, and Joseph knew that his stepfather, as he did every night, had gone to the parlor to read the newspaper while his mother washed the dishes. Joseph stared at the ceiling. He was still cold and tired, and his growling stomach just added to his misery.

Before he fell asleep, he heard a soft tap at his door. "It's me," said his older brother, Clay. "I knew you'd be hungry." He handed Joseph a hunk of roast pork and a piece of bread. "Sorry, this is all I could save for you," he whispered. He sat on the bed while Joseph wolfed down the leftovers.

"Thanks," Joseph said.

"Why did you get sent to your room?" Clay asked.

Quietly Joseph told his brother about his adventure at the river. Instead of the sympathy he expected, however, his brother nodded. "You deserved the punishment. That was a pretty stupid thing to do. And Mr. Byers warned you about it this morning. I heard him." Clay's voice softened. "Why don't you try to get along with Mr. Byers? It makes it hard on Mama when you don't."

"I hate him!" Joseph exclaimed. "You and Mama act like you don't even remember Papa."

Clay's usually calm voice snapped with anger. "I haven't forgotten him, not one bit. Neither has Mama. She cried for weeks after Papa died. Mr. Byers is not to blame for his death. I admit that he's kind of strict. Mama says he's not used to children. But he's not so bad if you give him a chance. He talked to Dr. Mercer for me. I still have to pass my Latin exam, but Dr. Mercer is going to interview me about being his apprentice."

"He's making everyone in town hate us," Joseph said. "First he's talking against slavery, and now he's even saying the states don't have a right to leave the Union."

"Everyone doesn't hate us," Clay said. "I think there're a lot of people thinking like Mr. Byers. They just aren't brave enough to admit it."

"Has he got you thinking his way?" Joseph asked. "Are you forgetting we lost the farm because Cyrus and Nate ran away? How can you feel sorry for any slaves? They waited until Mama was torn up with grief over Pa dying and needed their help the most. They didn't care about us at all."

Clay stood up. "Maybe they were afraid they'd never have another chance. Wouldn't you run away if you were a slave and thought you could escape?"

"We were good to them. Pa gave them land to grow their own vegetables. Mama made them two new shirts and pants every year."

"They were still slaves," Clay said quietly. "Listen, Mr. Byers gave me some pamphlets to read about slavery. You should look at them."

"I'm not reading any of his Yankee teaching," Joseph said, stubbornly shaking his head.

Clay was still angry when he left the room. Joseph curled up on his bed and thought about the conversation. Clay liked Mr. Byers because he was helping him secure a place with Dr. Mercer; his mother liked him because he allowed her to stay home with Jared, who needed a lot of care. For their sakes, Joseph would do whatever was expected to keep peace in the family. But he would never forget his real father, and he would never like Mr. Byers. "Never," he vowed silently.

Just before he drifted off to sleep, he remembered the cave he had seen at the mud slide. When he had told Clay the story of his afternoon adventures, he'd forgotten about it. Now he was glad. He would keep it a secret, he decided. As soon as it was safe, he would explore it by himself.

THREE

—◆—

A Warning

His stepfather was not at the table when Joseph came downstairs for breakfast the next morning. With a sigh of relief he slid onto his chair. Mrs. Byers was singing softly as she finished preparing breakfast. She gave him a sympathetic smile. "I imagine you are hungry. Are you feeling well?"

Joseph nodded. "My swim in the river doesn't seem to have hurt me any."

Clay was already at the table, spreading butter and jam on a warm soft biscuit. "It's not even daybreak. Why did Mr. Byers leave so early?" he asked his mother.

"Two more of the workers ran off to join the militia," Mrs. Byers answered with a worried look. "And there is still all the mess from the flood to clean up."

"My teacher at school told us that most of the militia will be joining up with the new Confederate army," Joseph said importantly. "There are seven states now that have withdrawn from the Union. The delegates are meeting in Alabama to pick the first president. She thinks it will be Jefferson Davis. Did you know he was born right here in Kentucky, just like President Lincoln?"

"Electing another president is ridiculous," said Clay. "Mr. Lincoln will never allow the states to leave the Union."

"How's he going to stop them?" Joseph asked from around a bite of fried ham. "Seems to me like it's too late. They've already voted themselves out of the Union."

"War," Clay answered. "It will be the northern states against the ones in the South."

Joseph shook his head. "Now that's pretty foolish. We can fight the British or the Spanish or another country. We can't go to war against ourselves! I don't much like Yankees, but I wouldn't want to shoot them."

"That's the whole idea," Clay said. "The states that seceded will be another country."

Joseph's eyes widened. He had never thought of it that way.

"I'm sure it won't come to that," said Mrs. Byers briskly. "I do feel sorry for Mr. Lincoln. He hasn't even been sworn in, and already he is facing all these problems. Whatever happens, talk is Kentucky will stay neutral. Thank heavens for that."

"You'd never know that if you went to town. The Confederates are by the courthouse, trying to get men to sign up for the militia. But down on Main Street the Union army is recruiting men, too. Everyone I know wants to fight. They say it's a matter of honor," Clay said. "The Yankees don't have a right to tell us how to live."

"Don't you even think about it," Mrs. Byers said fiercely. "You're only fourteen."

"Will Clary says he's going if there's fighting," Clay said. "He's only fourteen. He looks a lot older, though. He says those Confederate recruiters said you had to be eighteen, but he figures he can pass. I figure I can be more help if I learn some doctoring. There's bound to be a few people hurt." He frowned. "I suppose the fighting will be all over before I can help."

"If war comes, it might last a long time," their mother said. "Even right here in Branson Mills there are a lot of people sympathetic to the southern cause. Even if they don't believe in slavery, they believe it's our constitutional right to leave the Union. That's why I'm worried about Mr. Byers talking against slavery. I'm afraid he is making people angry."

"It's embarrassing," Joseph complained. With a defiant look at Clay he asked his mother, "You don't believe keeping slaves is wrong, do you?"

His mother frowned. "I don't know what to think anymore. I've been around slaves all my life. Why, I was practically raised by my auntie Millie. I loved her. And I was fond of Cyrus and Nate, too. Everyone I know who has slaves treats them kindly. They're like children, you know. I don't think they could take care of themselves if they were free."

"There are some free black people who live down the river not far from the mill," Clay reminded her. "I think their name is Douglass. They take care of themselves pretty well."

Joseph had seen the family when he had been exploring the river one day. There were a couple of kids about his own age, he remembered. Mr. Douglass made wooden chairs in a small workshop beside his house. There was a girl about thirteen named Hannah. Joseph saw her sometimes walking along the river to town to deliver wash her mother took in.

"They seem to do all right," Mrs. Byers said grudgingly. "But most of them can't even read or write."

Clay shrugged. "The pamphlets I read say they were beaten if they tried to learn. Besides, there're a lot of white people who can't read either."

Joseph folded his arms across his chest. "Pa wouldn't have had slaves if it was bad," he said. "He was the best man I know."

Mrs. Byers shook her head. "Your pa was a good man, and so is Mr. Byers." She rubbed her head as though it hurt. "I declare, I don't know who is right."

"Mr. Byers sounds like those Yankee abolitionists that were preaching in town awhile back," Joseph said. "The sheriff ran them out of town. I heard if they hadn't left when they did, some men were going to tar and feather them. That's what's going to happen to Mr. Byers if he's not careful."

Mrs. Byers looked at Joseph. "I won't have you talking disrespectful about Mr. Byers," she said sternly. She glanced at the parlor clock. "My goodness, it's getting late and Daisy isn't milked."

The morning milking was Joseph's job. Most people in town bought milk each day from farmers who came to town with crocks of it, and butter and eggs, but Mr. Byers had purchased a cow and chickens so that Jared would always have fresh dairy products. It was a chore Joseph never minded. Daisy was a gentle cow; she always stood quietly while Joseph milked, never kicking or switching her tail.

The barn was actually a small carriage house that was never used because Mr. Byers walked to his factory and back every day. Joseph turned Daisy out in the small pasture at one side while he shoveled out the stall and spread clean straw.

Clay had already left the house when Joseph came back inside. Branson Mills did not have a high school. Few students went past the sixth grade. With Mr. Byers's help, however, Clay had been accepted at a private school, the Branson Academy, at the other end of town. When his father had been alive, Joseph and Clay had gone to a country school that had only one room for all the grades. Now Joseph attended the Hill Street School. It was a fine brick building with a room for every level. Joseph was in the fifth grade, and his teacher was a lady named Miss Graham.

There was no sign of Zachary when he arrived at school. That did not surprise Joseph. He knew that Zachary's father often made him stay home and work at the mill. That was why Zachary was still in the third grade. Still, Joseph was disappointed. He had wanted to thank him again for the rescue.

Joseph had attended his new school for only a month, not long enough to make friends, but long enough that most of the other boys acted friendly. Today, however, a number of his classmates looked away when he came near, and no one smiled.

When he walked into the classroom, several of his classmates suddenly stopped talking and stared at him. He heard the word *abolitionist*. Joseph's face felt hot. He took his seat quickly and pretended to be busy looking at his spelling words. Everyone must have heard about Mr. Byers's yelling at the minister. They probably thought Joseph felt the same way.

He ate lunch by himself, and when he returned to class, he found his way blocked. "I heard your stepfather is a Yankee spy," Andrew said with a scowl. Andrew was a good head taller than Joseph. He was hotheaded and often in trouble for fighting. Joseph tried to ignore him and return to his desk, but Andrew shook his fist under Joseph's nose. "Maybe you're a spy too."

"I'm not a spy, and neither is Mr. Byers," Joseph sputtered, angry that he was forced to defend his stepfather. "He just doesn't think people should have slaves."

"What do you think?" Andrew asked.

"We used to have slaves. I don't see anything wrong with it," Joseph answered.

The faces around him suddenly looked a little more friendly. Andrew let him pass. "We don't need any Yankee abolitionists around here telling us what to do. But I guess you can't help how your stepfather talks," he said.

Joseph shook his head. Feeling a little bolder, he added, "I don't even like my stepfather."

The afternoon went better. Although no one really talked to him, at least several of his classmates smiled.

Even though the next day was Friday, school was closed for the Branson Mills Centennial Celebration. There were going to be games and contests and horse races in the afternoons. Everyone cheered when Miss Graham announced that in honor of the centennial she would not give out any homework. Excited by the prospect of three whole days of freedom, the class scrambled out the door.

"You'd better tell you stepfather to quit talking against having slaves," Andrew warned as he ran off to join some friends. "There're a lot of people in town getting mighty unhappy with him."

Joseph walked home alone. The idea of telling Mr. Byers to do anything, let alone to stop talking against slavery, almost made him smile.

It was too nice a day to ruin by thinking about

slavery or war. Instead, he thought about the celebration. Miss Graham had talked about how much the town had grown in one hundred years. At first there had been only a few houses and a mill owned by a man named Branson, who some folks said was related to Daniel Boone himself. It was the same mill that Zachary Young's father owned now. The town might have stayed just a small settlement, but then the canal was built. It had made Branson Mills an important shipping hub, sending rice, indigo, cotton, and tobacco to the Ohio River and from there all over the country. Now most goods were shipped by train, and the town boasted many shops and comfortable houses with shady tree-lined streets.

Joseph looked at the sky. It was perfect weather for a celebration. Although February was often cold and wintry, today was mild. The sun was shining, and the sky a perfect blue.

Joseph had never been to a centennial celebration before, of course, but he imagined it would be just like the county fair, except there would be speeches and maybe even fireworks. An instant of sadness washed over him as he remembered last

September's fair. His father had still been alive then. His mother had grown a giant pumpkin. It was so big his father and Clay could hardly lift it into the wagon. He remembered the laughter as they finally had to roll it up a ramp. "Queen of pumpkins," his father had called his mother. That pumpkin had won first prize, and the mayor himself had bought it. He had told Joseph's mother he was going to have his cook, a slave woman known as Aunt Bea, make him pumpkin pies all winter.

Joseph thought about Aunt Bea. Did she hate being a slave? She never seemed to mind. Every time Joseph saw her, she was smiling.

"Tarnation," Joseph said out loud. "There you go, thinking about slavery again."

Mr. Byers seemed to have forgotten his anger of the night before. He smiled at Joseph when he returned home from work. "Well, are you all ready to go to the centennial tomorrow?"

Joseph nodded. "Yes, sir."

Having greeted Joseph, his new stepfather seemed at a loss for something else to say.

While they ate dinner, Mr. and Mrs. Byers talked about the celebration. "I think all four thousand people in town are going tomorrow. People are afraid there won't be any more social events if this trouble keeps growing," said Mr. Byers.

Joseph watched in amazement at the amount of meat, potatoes, applesauce, and beans Clay piled on his plate. Clay had been growing at an alarming rate the last year, and his mother joked that he must have a hollow leg to hold all that food. Joseph wished he would start growing like that. No matter how much he ate, he remained skinny. From across the table Jared grinned at Joseph. He looked better than usual, and he ate nearly everything on his plate. Jared was only six. His hair was red, like Joseph's. But Jared's hair was softly curled, and Joseph's was straight.

Joseph was glad that Jared was feeling well enough to go to the celebration. His little brother had little enough fun. Mrs. Byers often had to hang the white cloth over the fence as a sign to Dr. Mercer that he was needed.

After dinner Clay went back to his studies, and Joseph played a game of checkers with Jared in the parlor.

"There is an arts and crafts contest at the celebration. You should enter your carvings," Mr. Byers said, putting down his new issue of *Harper's Monthly Magazine.*

Joseph looked up from his game. He was surprised that Mr. Byers even knew about the drawerful of tiny animals Joseph had carved with the knife his real father had given him the year before.

In spite of his resolution not to like Mr. Byers, Joseph couldn't help the pleased smile that crossed his face. "Do you think I should?"

"I do," said Mr. Byers, also smiling. "They really are excellent."

Joseph shrugged. "Maybe I will."

Mr. Byers went back to his magazine. Joseph thought about the carvings he could enter. He would take only the best ones.

Suddenly Jared giggled. Joseph looked back to his game just as Jared jumped three more of his pieces.

"I win, I win," he crowed.

Mr. Byers looked up from his reading again and beamed at Jared. No one could doubt that Mr. Byers loved his youngest stepson. Jared left the game and climbed up onto his stepfather's lap. "Read me a story," he begged.

Mr. Byers picked up a book of fairy tales. The warm glow Joseph had felt at the unexpected praise disappeared, leaving a pang of jealously. Before Mr. Byers had come along, Joseph had been the one to read to Jared. He picked up the checker pieces and angrily shoved them into their box for safekeeping. Mr. Byers looked up at the noise with a puzzled look. Joseph stormed out of the room. It was too bad people could not do the same thing as the states, he thought. He would secede from any family with Mr. Byers in it.

FOUR

Celebration!

"Is it time to go?" Jared asked the next morning, for at least the fourth time since breakfast.

"Almost ready," Mrs. Byers answered patiently. "Don't get yourself too excited." She cast a worried look at him while she tucked a clean white cloth over the lunch in the picnic basket.

Jared, however, could not sit still. He wiggled impatiently in his chair. Joseph felt just as anxious as his brother. He was nearly eleven years old, though, and knew better than to keep asking. Still, he wished his mother would hurry.

The sky was a clear bright blue, and the air was crisp but not cold. Joseph peeked at the clock in the parlor. It was almost ten o'clock, he saw with dismay.

At last Mrs. Byers untied her apron and put on her hat. "I'm ready," she announced.

Mr. Byers and Clay stomped into the kitchen. Ordinarily they would have walked to the fairgrounds. It was only two miles away. However, because of Jared and the huge picnic basket, Mr. Byers had rented a carriage and two horses to pull it. The carriage was shiny black with a stylish gold stripe. Mr. Byers had rented it from Mr. Curtis, who owned the livery stable in town.

Joseph held the box of carvings he'd selected in his lap. He was entering his best pieces—a bear, a deer, and the eagle he had hoped to mount on the driftwood that had gotten him into so much trouble. Even without the mounting Joseph was especially proud of that one. It had taken more than a month to finish. Mr. Johnson, who had a general store, kept some of Joseph's carvings on display and sometimes sold one. A Yankee from Cincinnati had once given Joseph twenty-five dollars for one that wasn't half as good as the eagle he was taking to the contest.

Mr. Byers was a tall, broad-shouldered man who handled the horses with assurance. His long, bushy mustache was carefully waxed on the ends to make it curl up. He slapped the reins, and the horses pranced smartly down the road.

"It's a good day for the celebration," Jared said happily.

"I probably won't get to see much," Clay complained. "I have a job selling lemonade." Then he brightened. "But I'm getting paid two whole dollars." He fell silent, thinking of ways to spend his fortune.

The road was clogged with traffic heading for the fairgrounds. Ladies in wide hoopshirts strolled down the wooden sidewalks, holding up their skirts to keep them out of the dust and dirt. The carriage rumbled over the main street of town. Branson Mills was proud of this road: It was paved with a macadam surface. The side roads had not been paved yet. They were only dirt and were so deeply rutted and slippery with mud when it rained that they were nearly impassable.

At the fairgrounds the air nearly crackled with excitement. Some of the farmers had brought prize animals to show, just as they would for the county fair. A large group of men were having a tug-of-war contest while onlookers cheered for their favorites. In a clearing another crowd, sitting on benches, watched a fiddle contest. Even from this distance the cheerful music made Joseph want to tap his feet.

Jared's mouth made a little oh of surprise. He had never seen so many people.

Just seeing Jared's excitement made Joseph happy. Poor Jared had little enough fun in his life. Joseph draped an arm around his brother's shoulder. "This afternoon there will be horse races," he said. "That's what I like."

The racetrack was off to one side of the fairgrounds. There was a brand-new grandstand, but Joseph preferred to watch from the grass around the track.

An American flag with thirty-three stars flew from the top of the horse barns. Joseph studied it as the carriage rolled by. What would they do if all those states really did leave the Union? They would have to make a whole new flag. The thought made him feel strangely empty.

On the other side of the barns and sheds was a shady meadow with a pond, perfect for picnics.

Mr. Byers paid the ten cents' admission for each of them, grumbling good-naturedly about high prices.

Clay jumped from the carriage as soon as they were inside the gates and hurried off to his job. He took Joseph's box of carvings. "I'll drop these off at the crafts judging for you," he promised.

"There's Mayor Cooper," Mrs. Byers said, waving gaily.

The mayor was standing near the gate. He tipped his tall stovepipe hat at Joseph's mother. The buttons on his coat stretched across his round belly.

"I hope you're growing another pumpkin for the fair this year," Mayor Cooper said in a hearty voice. "That is, if there *is* a fair this year," he added with a dark look at Mr. Byers, as though he would be personally responsible if there weren't.

Joseph's stepfather ignored the mayor and guided the horses and carriage through the crowds toward the picnic area. "Mayor Cooper is a fool," he said. "If he had his way, Kentucky would leave the Union with the rest of the South."

"Would that really be so terrible?" Mrs. Byers asked timidly.

Her husband pulled in the reins and twisted in his seat to look at her. "Kentucky is on the border between the North and the South. If there is a war, which state do you think will be crushed first? North or South. Whichever side we are on, the other will attack. Our only chance is to remain neutral."

"Oh," Mrs. Byers said quietly. "I never thought of that." She was silent as her husband found a shady spot to leave the horses.

Joseph thought about his stepfather's words. He had to admit they made sense.

"Let's not think about war today," Mrs. Byers said as they walked back to the midway. "Let's just enjoy the celebration."

Mr. Byers patted her shoulder. "You're right," he said, smiling. "Today we'll just enjoy ourselves."

It was a promise he could not keep for long. As they approached the grandstand, they passed a large group of businessmen from town having a heated discussion near a platform where a very large lady was singing Stephen Foster's "Jeannie with the Light Brown Hair." One of the men called to Mr. Byers. A few of the faces in the group were openly hostile, but others seemed friendly enough. As usual the conversation was about the new president. "Ugliest fellow you ever saw," said Mr. Taggert, who owned a dry goods store.

"I thought you admired Mr. Lincoln," said Mr. Byers.

"I do," answered Mr. Taggert. "Fine man. Heard him speak once. He's a tall, skinny fellow, and his wife is short and plump. Some people say she's secretly sympathetic to the South. I sure don't envy Mr. Lincoln. He stepped into a whole mess of problems."

"The only reason Mr. Lincoln won was that the Democrats were divided with three candidates," said Mr. Johnson. "If the Democrats had just picked one strong candidate, he wouldn't have won."

"None of the southern states voted for him." Mr. Lippit, who owned the bookstore, joined the conversation. "That's another reason they should be allowed to secede."

"We can't allow every state with a disagreement to secede," said Mr. Byers. "Soon there wouldn't be any country."

Joseph stood on one foot, then the other. He was bored, but he didn't dare interrupt when grown-ups were talking.

At last Mr. Byers reached into his pocket and handed Joseph some coins. "Here's twenty-five cents," he said. "Spend it wisely," he admonished. "And be back at the picnic grove at two or you'll miss your dinner."

Joseph's fingers curled around the coins. He could hardly believe his good fortune. Twenty-five cents just to spend on himself!

"May I go with Joseph?" Jared asked.

Mrs. Byers started to say no, but her husband nodded. "See to it that you watch your brother," he told Joseph sternly. "Don't let him get overly tired."

"Yes, sir," Joseph said. Pulling Jared by the hand, he made his escape.

"What do you want to see first?" he asked Jared.

"Sheep," Jared answered immediately.

They found the sheep barn easily, and Jared

reached through the rail fencing to pet one. The sheep looked at Jared with calm eyes and started nibbling on his shirt. Jared laughed and pulled his arm away.

The fiddlers had stopped for a while, and now a band was playing. The boys wandered out of the sheep barn and watched a clown juggling balls.

Just then Joseph saw some boys he recognized from school. "They're starting games over by the picnic grove," one of them announced.

"Do you want to go?" Joseph said, turning to ask Jared. His brother was not behind him, as he'd thought. At last he spotted him standing on the bottom rail of a fenced-off pen. Inside was a bull with the longest horns Joseph had ever seen. Beside Jared stood a tall boy with a thatch of unruly brown hair.

"Zachary," Joseph shouted.

Zachary grinned, showing a broken front tooth. "Well, well, it's the mud boy."

"I never got a chance to really thank you," Joseph said.

Zachary looked embarrassed. "Wasn't much. Just pulled on a rope."

Jared was looking through the fence at the bull. "Can I pet him?"

"No, you can't," Joseph said, grabbing his brother's arm.

"That bull came all the way from Texas," Zachary informed them. "He looks mean, but I heard he's as gentle as a kitten."

"I don't think I want to find out," Joseph said. "We're going over to the games. Want to come?"

Zachary shrugged and fell into step beside them. They passed by a row of wagons, each with good smells. Outside each the vendors shouted out their offerings. "Goober peas, fresh roasted goober peas," cried one.

Joseph spotted Clay and waved. "Iced lemonade," Clay bellowed.

Mrs. Byers was standing near the wagon, drinking a cup of lemonade. Joseph was surprised to see her alone. Then he spied Mr. Byers a few feet away. He was deep in conversation with two rough-looking men. There was something threatening about them and the way they were standing too close to Mr. Byers. His stepfather was shaking his head. He looked angry. Joseph was too far away to hear what was being said, but he could see that passersby were giving the men curious looks. Finally Mr. Byers brushed past the two men and, taking his wife by the arm, walked away. When Joseph looked back, the two men had melted away into the crowd.

Jared was tugging at his jacket. "Joseph, Joseph," he cried, pointing to the next wagon. A man was dipping apples into a steaming pot of melted caramel.

Zachary was looking at him curiously. "Is something wrong?" he asked quietly.

Joseph shrugged off the feeling of foreboding and walked to the apple wagon. He looked behind once more, but his parents were no longer in sight.

"Ten cents," said the man when Joseph asked the price.

Joseph hesitated. If he bought two apples, his money would be nearly gone. "I'll buy one, and we can share it," he told Jared.

Zachary looked away, and Joseph realized he didn't have any money. He bought a second apple and handed it to Zachary.

Zachary seemed amazed, as though no one had

ever done anything nice for him before. He wolfed down the apple as though he were afraid Joseph might change his mind. Joseph and Jared ate theirs more slowly, savoring its sticky sweetness.

"The three-legged race is about to start," Zachary said, pointing to a line of boys. "Want to try it with me?"

"Stay right here," Joseph ordered Jared, pointing to a rock. Obediently Jared sat down. From there he would have a good view of the race.

Joseph and Zachary stepped up to the starting line, and a man tied one of Joseph's legs to one of Zachary's.

"We have to move together," Zachary said. "Let's start with the tied-together leg."

"Go," shouted the announcer.

They took the first step, then stumbled on the second. Laughing, they picked themselves up. Several other pairs were on the ground too.

"Ready?" Zachary asked.

Joseph forgot and started out with his free leg, and down they tumbled again.

"Maybe we should just roll to the finish line," Joseph said between laughs. They tried to untangle themselves, but it was too late. The first pair of boys crossed the line.

"Too bad," Joseph said. "If we'd been able to practice for a few minutes, we might've had a chance."

"Next, the greased pig chase," the announcer yelled.

Joseph glanced over at Jared. He was sitting right where they had left him, grinning as though he was enjoying himself.

The pig was pink and slick with oil. It squealed as the cage was carried to the middle of the field. The contestants made a wide ring around the pen, and the announcer lifted the gate. There followed a mad dash of slippery pig, squeals, yelling boys, and laughing audience. Twice Joseph had his arm around the wiggling porker, and twice the pig struggled free. Zachary was having no better luck. Some of the boys were laughing too hard even to try.

At last a boy named George whom Joseph knew from school threw himself over the pig and managed to hold on by wrapping both arms and legs around the worn-out creature.

"The winner!" the announcer crowed. The on-lookers cheered and laughed.

Joseph fell back on the ground exhausted. Zachary collapsed beside him. "I thought I had him once," Joseph exclaimed.

"Just as well we didn't win," Zachary said. "The prize is the pig." He pointed to George, who was proudly carrying his prize away. "His mother will not be pleased to keep a pig in her garden."

Joseph laughed. "That was fun. I wish Jared could do things like that." He rolled over and looked at the spot where Jared had been at the start of the chase. Then he sat up quickly. His brother was nowhere in sight.

FIVE

———— • ————

A Daring Rescue

After the first moment of panic Joseph sat down and tried to think.

"He can't have gone far," Zachary said. "Maybe he went to your carriage for something to eat."

Hannah Douglass, the girl who carried wash back and forth for her mother, was standing by herself, watching the games. "Are you looking for your little brother?" she asked.

Joseph nodded.

"I saw him walking back toward the barns," she said.

Suddenly Joseph knew where his brother had gone. "The bull. You told him it was gentle," he said accusingly.

Zachary looked stricken. "I was joking."

The boys set off at a dead run. They passed the vendors still singing their chants. People stared as they pushed through the crowds. At last the pen was in sight. Joseph stopped, sighing with relief. No small boy clung to the fence. He turned to go when Zachary suddenly grabbed his arm. "He's inside the pen," he gasped.

Joseph moaned. He could see Jared now. He had crawled through the fence and was walking toward the bull. The bull pawed the ground nervously, his horns lowered. No one else seemed to notice what was happening.

Joseph started toward the fence, but Zachary grabbed his arm. "Let me circle around and get his attention. Then you grab Jared."

Joseph nodded. Zachary raced in a wide circle around the pen. The bull snorted loudly, and for the first time Jared looked nervous. He looked back at the fence and spotted Joseph.

"I don't think he likes me," Jared said.

"Step backward very slowly," Joseph said. He kept his gaze riveted on the bull, but out of the corner of his eye he saw that Zachary was climbing the fence behind the animal.

Jared took one slow step backward, and Joseph squeezed under the lowest rail. He inched his way over to Jared, keeping his eyes on the bull. The bull twitched with annoyance as a big fly landed on his back. He pawed the dust with one hoof and watched the boys.

Careful not to make any sudden movements, Joseph reached for Jared. He nodded to Zachary, signaling that he was in position. Immediately Zachary took off his hat and waved it. Hey, bull," he screamed. "Over here."

For one brief moment the bull was distracted. He turned toward the new irritation, snorting with anger. Joseph's fingers tightened around his brother's arm.

"There's a child in the bull's pen!" a lady screamed.

The bull seemed to rear up in the air as he wheeled back toward the boys. "Run," shouted Zachary.

Joseph did not need to be told. Gripping his brother's arm, he yanked Jared off his feet and in one motion threw him under the fence. He dived after him, rolling free just as the bull hit the fence with a loud thump that seemed as though it would break the rails. The fence held, however, and Joseph stood up, still shaking. He helped his brother to his feet. "Are you all right?" he asked.

Jared nodded, but his face was white under his freckles.

Joseph saw that Hannah had followed them. She smiled shyly. "That was the bravest thing I ever saw," she said.

Embarrassed, Joseph shrugged. "Not really. I was scared to death."

Zachary ran around the fence and patted his back. "That was one bad-tempered bull!" he exclaimed.

Joseph's knees were weak at the thought of what could have happened. A small crowd was gathering. Suddenly worried that his parents would hear the commotion, Joseph grabbed Jared and slipped away from the well-wishers. They lost themselves among the food vendors' wagons.

"Don't tell Mama I went in the bull's pen," Jared pleaded.

"I won't," Joseph promised. "Don't you tell that I lost you."

"I'm sorry I didn't wait like you told me," Jared said seriously. "I was just going to pet the bull and come right back."

"Here's a good rule to remember," Zachary said. "Never pet anything with three-foot horns."

They walked to the picnic grounds. Joseph saw with relief that his mother was busily laying out the dinner on a blanket. She was humming to herself as she worked. Obviously she had not heard about Jared's narrow escape. Mr. Byers was nearby tending the horses.

"There you are," she said. "I was beginning to think we would have to eat up all this food ourselves."

"This is my friend Zachary," Joseph said. "He's the one who saved me the other night."

Mrs. Byers wrapped her arms around Zachary and hugged him so long he squirmed with embarrassment. "Thank you for saving my son," she said simply.

Zachary's face flamed bright red. "Wasn't much," he said. He ducked his head and drew a circle in the dirt with his toe.

"Would you like to eat with us?" Mrs. Byers asked.

Zachary hesitated. "It looks mighty good."

"Then it's settled," Mrs. Byers said. She handed him a plate filled with fried chicken, corn bread, and baked beans. For dessert there was cherry pie.

Clay came jogging up to the carriage, looking with hunger at all the food. "I just have a few minutes before I get back to work. Did you see all that excitement?" he asked around bites. "Somebody told me that a little boy was attacked by a bull."

"Oh, dear," Mrs. Byers said. "Is he all right?"

Clay gave Joseph and Zachary a suspicious look. "It seems that two other boys saved him."

"I wish we could have seen that," Joseph said, trying to sound innocent. "It must have been exciting."

The picnic grounds were getting crowded as more and more families came to eat. Mr. Byers finished graining the horses and joined them for the meal. He looked surprised to see Zachary, but when Mrs. Byers explained, he shook Zachary's hand. "That was a fine rescue. Joseph told us all about it," he said warmly.

Jared finished his meal and leaned up against his mother. "I'm tired," he said sleepily.

"Why don't you take a little nap before we go back?" said Mrs. Byers. She fetched an old blanket from the carriage and wrapped it around him.

"I didn't like that bad bull," Jared murmured as he drifted off to sleep.

Mr. Byers gave Joseph a hard look. "What bull is he talking about?"

Clay stared at Joseph. "It was you!"

Mrs. Byers's hands flew to her face. "Jared was the boy in the bull's pen?" she gasped.

"It was my fault," Zachary said. "I told him the bull was gentle."

Mr. Byers frowned at Joseph. "I am proud of you for saving your brother. Yet I wonder how it happened in the first place if you had been taking care of him like you were told."

Joseph hung his head. "I didn't. I was trying to catch the greased pig."

"And you were deceitful about it," scolded Joseph's mother.

Clay gave Joseph a sympathetic look. "I have to get back to work," he said, handing his mother the empty plate.

Mrs. Byers placed the dishes and remaining food back in the basket. Her husband picked up Jared and tucked him into the carriage with the blanket. "The races will be starting soon, but Jared is tired," he said. "Since you didn't tend to your brother earlier, you can do it now."

Joseph bit his lip in disappointment as his mother and Mr. Byers strolled back to the fairgrounds. Joseph sat down on the ground and leaned his back against one of the carriage wheels. He looked at Zachary. "You'd better hurry or you'll miss the start of the races."

Zachary sat down beside him and shrugged. "I'll stay with you."

Zachary was a true friend, Joseph thought. He looked out over the picnic grounds. They were nearly empty now as families headed toward the racetrack. Two Quaker families, the men in their broad-brimmed hats, the women in dark clothes, lingered together some distance away. Joseph recognized Mr. Baker, who owned a small furniture store in town. He had a strange manner of speaking; he used words like *thee* and *thou*. His son David was in Joseph's room at school, but Joseph didn't know him very well.

Suddenly two rough-looking men on horseback rode into the picnic clearing. They galloped over to Joseph and Zachary. "We're looking for an escaped slave," one of them said. "Seen any black folk around you don't know?"

It was the two men he'd seen earlier in the day talking to his stepfather. Joseph shook his head. "No, sir," he said politely.

The man stared at Zachary. "How about you?"

"Nope," Zachary said shortly.

The men wheeled their horses and rode over toward the Quaker families.

"Maybe we ought to go look for the slave. Might be some reward money," Zachary said.

Joseph shrugged. "How would we catch him even if we did find him?" he asked. "Anyway, he's probably halfway to the Ohio River by now. And I have to stay here with Jared, remember?"

Zachary nodded and spit on the ground. "A lot of Yankees help them escape. They don't even care that their owners probably paid a lot of money for them."

Joseph did not reply. He was watching the slave catchers. Mr. Baker was standing up, facing the two horsemen. Then the two men circled him. They were shouting, but Joseph was too far away to hear what. Mr. Baker was shaking his head. Then one of the men took something off the saddle of his horse. It was a long black whip. The man let it drag along the ground, a silent threat as he talked. Again Mr. Baker shook his head. The man with the whip made a quick motion with his wrist, and the whip cracked in a threatening manner.

"Why are they being so rough with Mr. Baker?" Joseph asked.

"Sometimes Quakers help the slaves escape," Zachary said quietly. "My pa claims almost all of them are abolitionists."

Watching the two men bully the Quaker made Joseph feel uncomfortable. He looked at the fairground, hoping someone would come along. But the two men seemed tired of their cruel game, or perhaps they finally believed Mr. Baker. The man with the whip snapped it in the air again with a loud CRACK! Then they galloped away. As soon as they were gone, the Quakers quickly gathered their belongings and hurried away.

Joseph walked over to the carriage and peeked at Jared, still sleeping soundly.

"Hey, mud boy," Zachary said in a teasing voice. "It's getting late, and Pa will be mad if I don't get my chores done. I'd better get home. I had a good time today." With a friendly wave he was off.

Joseph sat down on a nearby boulder. The picnic grounds were completely empty now except for Jared and him. The races had started. Joseph could hear the crowd cheering. The afternoon dragged slowly on, and still Jared slept. It was not until the races were over and the sun was low in the sky that he finally awoke and sat up, rubbing his eyes. Then he climbed out of the carriage, still looking tired in spite of his nap. Joseph saw the rest of his family heading back.

Clay was holding the box of Joseph's carvings. "Your eagle won a blue ribbon," Clay announced.

Mr. Byers handed him a ribbon and coins.

"There was a prize of three dollars. I'm sorry that your punishment kept you from being there to receive it," he said as the family climbed in for the trip back to the livery stable.

Joseph sat down glumly and did not speak. His mother gave him a sympathetic look. "Everyone was amazed at how nice they were."

"You have more money than I do, and I worked all day," Clay said, obviously trying to make him feel better.

Joseph was so unhappy that he forgot to tell his family about the two strangers and their hunt until they had turned in the carriage and were walking home, Jared safely perched on his stepfather's back.

"Since Congress passed the Fugitive Slave Law, bounty hunters can go to any state, slave or free, to bring them back," Mr. Byers said grimly. "I even saw a poster warning free black people to be careful because there have been cases where the bounty hunters have kidnapped them to sell them in the Deep South. Of course no one believes them when they say they are free."

Joseph was only half-listening to his stepfather. He was tired of thinking about slavery and war.

Let the grown-ups concern themselves with things like that. For himself, he had enough things to worry about. There was a new home, a new school, a stepfather he didn't like, and a father's face that was fading away when he closed his eyes and tried to remember it at night.

SIX

—◆—

A Day at Home

The next morning Joseph did the milking quickly and brought the pail in the house. He covered it with a cloth to let it cool and give the cream time to rise to the top.

His mother placed a platter of fried cornmeal mush and maple syrup and another of thickly sliced fried ham on the table for breakfast. Clay clumped downstairs. He yawned and stretched as he sat down for breakfast.

Mr. Byers took a bite. "Delicious," he announced. "Fit for a king."

Joseph's mother looked pleased at the compliment.

"I need to do some washing today," she said. "But later I might go shopping. We're out of sugar. And I need fifty cents to pay for the shoes I had repaired."

Mr. Byers handed her several silver dollars. "Why don't you let me hire Mrs. Douglass to do the washing for you?"

Mrs. Byers shook her head. "I don't mind doing it. And with things slow at your factory it doesn't seem right. Everything's so expensive these days."

"If a war comes, things will be even more expensive," Mr. Byers remarked.

"Do you really think there'll be a war?" asked Mrs. Byers.

Joseph had been only half-listening to the conversation, but at the word *war* he looked up. Mr. Byers was nodding. "Mr. Lincoln has already said he won't let the country be torn apart. Tempers are so high it won't take much to start fighting. All this marching and singing going on." Mr. Byers shook his head. "Most folks are acting like it's a picnic instead of a war."

"I don't think I would have voted for Mr. Lincoln," said Mrs. Byers thoughtfully. "If the southern states want to leave the Union, he should just let them."

"Fortunately for the country women can't vote." He chuckled. "What do women know of government?"

Mrs. Byers said nothing, but instead of singing the way she usually did when she did dishes, she rattled the pots and pans as she cleared the table, and Joseph knew she was unhappy. He thought his stepfather was wrong. His mother often helped him with his studies. She had helped him memorize the Declaration of Independence, and she hadn't needed to look at a book. She already knew every word by heart.

Mr. Byers looked at Joseph. "Clay is talking to Dr. Mercer today. You stay home and help your mother. If she doesn't need you, there are logs that need to be split for the stove."

Joseph's shoulders drooped. He had planned to explore the cave.

"I might leave work a little early," Mr. Byers said. "I hear there's going to be a small slave auction by the courthouse."

Mrs. Byers looked worried. "Maybe you should

stay away," she said. "There're too many people upset with you already."

"When people are upset, they are more likely to think," said Mr. Byers. "Maybe some of them will realize how truly evil it is for one man to own another." In an unusual display of affection he kissed his wife's cheek. "Don't worry. I can take care of myself."

Clay, looking handsome but uncomfortable in a new suit, left for his interview with Dr. Mercer. Joseph headed outside to start on the wood splitting.

"Fetch me water for the clothes washing first, Joseph," Mrs. Byers said as he reached for the door.

Joseph pumped several buckets of water. His mother heated a huge tubful on the stove while she sorted the clothes. First she would wash the whites, scrubbing them on a ribbed washboard. Next the colored things would be washed in the same water. Then Joseph would have to bring in more for the rinsing. After that the tub would be filled once more, and his mother would boil the clothes, stirring them with a wooden paddle. When they were finished, she would hang the clothes outside to dry. It was a job that took her most of the day.

While his mother worked, Joseph tackled the wood. The logs, from a tree cut last spring, had been seasoning near the barn. It was good hickory. Hickory logs were hard, which meant they burned for a long time. Their hardness also made them difficult to split. Joseph had to stand each log on its end and pound in a wedge to force them to crack.

Joseph worked for several hours, making a satisfying pile of wood ready for the stove. After so long his stomach was growling with hunger. As he walked to the house, he rubbed the palm of his hand, where blisters had formed.

The kitchen was humid from the washing. Mrs. Byers was lifting each piece of steaming hot clothing with a wooden paddle and putting it into another tub on the floor near the stove. Joseph knew she would let them cool long enough so that she could wring out the water before hanging them outside.

"I'm hungry," Joseph announced.

Mrs. Byers left the clothes to cool and made a

lunch. "I don't like to leave Jared when he's feeling so sick," she said as she put lunch on a tray for Jared to eat in bed. "I'd like you to do the errands for me."

Joseph nodded happily. Here was his chance to look at the cave. The ground would be dry by now. He glanced at the clock in the parlor. He could make a quick visit to the cave and still have time to do his mother's errands.

A brisk wind outside promised a return to winter weather. Joseph pulled his coat around him as he walked quickly to the river.

The ground was dry enough for him to climb down the bank, even though the mud slide had made it steeper than before. The river had gone down to its normal depth, no more than waist high. Joseph could hardly believe it was the same river that had nearly drowned him a few days before. The entrance to the cave was narrow, but when he peeked inside, he could see a rather large cavern. He crawled through the entrance, wishing he had thought to bring a lantern. The top of the cavern was high enough that he could stand quite comfortably. Stepping carefully, he examined the area. It was the size of a small room. At one side he noticed another opening. Maybe the whole hillside was a huge network of caverns. Feeling along cautiously, he stepped into the second passageway. But away from the outside entrance it was impossible to see. He retraced his steps and squeezed out into the daylight.

He would share his discovery with Zachary, he decided. They could return with ropes and lanterns and explore the rest of the cave. Excited at the idea, he looked at the opening. It would be visible to anyone coming down the river. He climbed up the bank and gathered enough brush to screen the cave. When he was done, he climbed down to the river and checked. If anyone looked carefully, he'd see the cave, but with the brush in place no one would give it more than a passing glance. Dusting off the dirt from his clothes, he climbed back up the hill and hurried toward town.

The shoe repair shop was tucked into a narrow alley behind the main street. He handed the proprietor fifty cents and waited while the man hunted for the right shoes among the piles on every shelf. Suddenly he heard shouts from outside. He stepped to the door and peeked.

Several young men wearing the blue uniform of

the Union army were backed up against the wall, facing an angry crowd of other young men. Joseph recognized several of them: They were trouble-makers who generally hung around town drinking and fighting. One of them shook his fist at a soldier. "Why don't you get on home, Yankee? We don't need you telling us what we can't do."

"I'm no Yankee. I come from Kentucky just like you," the soldier protested, "but I don't think states can just break up the country anytime they feel like it."

The cobbler tapped Joseph on the shoulder. "Found them!" he exclaimed.

Joseph stepped back into the shop and waited impatiently while the cobbler tied the shoes together with string. "Pay no attention to that outside," he said, jerking his head. "There're fights like that almost every day now."

Joseph nodded and stepped back out the door. The men were brawling now, seemingly evenly matched. As Joseph watched, a Union officer astride a big black horse rode into the alley. He pulled his gun out of his side holster, and Joseph caught his breath. The officer merely fired in the air and the men froze, wiping bloody noses with the backs of their hands. A second later the local boys had run off and the soldiers were stumbling out of the alley under the officer's watchful eye.

Joseph's next errand was to purchase two pounds of sugar. He crossed the street, heading for the general store.

The clock on the courthouse tower said two. There was a small crowd gathered nearby. He remembered what his stepfather had said about a slave auction. Curious, he walked toward the crowd. Zachary was there, standing on the corner by himself. He spotted Joseph and waved. Leaving the sugar purchase for later, Joseph hurried to his friend.

"Is it the slave auction?" Joseph asked.

When Zachary nodded, Joseph grabbed his arm and pulled him toward some bushes growing at the side of the courthouse. Crouched behind, they had a good view.

"Mr. Byers said he might come," Joseph whispered. "I don't want him to see me."

Zachary stood up and peered over the crowd. About thirty people had gathered for the auction, but there was no sign of Mr. Byers.

A platform had been raised behind the courthouse, and the crowd was gathered around it. A young strong-looking black man was on it. He stood quietly, eyes downward, while an auctioneer praised his abilities. "John here is a good blacksmith. You can hire him out, and he'll practically pay for himself."

A man from the watching crowd climbed up onto the platform. He felt John's muscles, made him open his mouth, and looked at his teeth. "One thousand dollars," said the man as he climbed down.

Joseph watched in shocked silence. Of course he knew about slave auctions, but he'd never actually seen one. Had Pa bought his slaves in just such a way? Had he coldly looked at their teeth as if they were no more than horses? Still, he told himself, slaves were expensive. His father would have made sure the ones he bought were healthy.

Next to the platform were two young girls. One was no more than fourteen. Tears streamed down her cheeks as she stood with her arms around a younger girl, who was sobbing openly.

"Their mother has already been sold," Zachary whispered. "The new owner didn't want the girls."

"That seems mean," Joseph remarked.

Zachary looked at him and shrugged. "They're slaves. They don't feel things like we do."

"Then why are they crying like that?" Joseph asked.

The bidding for John stopped at fifteen hundred, and the new owner, the one who had examined John's teeth, paid and led him away. The girls were then prodded until they climbed the platform, still clinging to each other. "Lily has had some training to be a housemaid. Mariam, her younger sister, is already a good seamstress. You can buy them both, or I'll sell them separate," said the auctioneer.

Mariam sagged weakly against her sister. "Please, no," she begged. The crowd ignored her distress. Lily stood stiffly, awaiting her fate.

Suddenly Joseph saw a familiar figure. Mr. Byers strode up to the platform and faced the crowd. Several people booed when they saw him, but Joseph's stepfather stood firmly in front of them, his eyes blazing. "You should be ashamed of yourselves. All of you. These are human beings, and even worse, these two are children."

Several men in the crowd jeered. "Mind your

own business! Get him out of here!" Someone picked up a rock and threw it.

Joseph feared for his stepfather. He looked around for someone to help. A few people looked ashamed, but no one made a move.

"Hold it there, Henry," Sheriff Underwood said, stepping out of the crowd. "Right or wrong, these people aren't breaking the law. If you don't leave, I'll have to arrest you."

Mr. Byers allowed the sheriff to lead him away, but he called back a final challenge: "How can you sleep at night and do this?"

Joseph did not wait to see the bidding begin again. He pushed his way out of the bushes and ran back down the street.

Zachary caught up with him at the door of the general store.

"What's wrong?" Zachary asked. "Why did you run away like that?"

"I've got to do some chores for my mother," Joseph answered.

Zachary stared at him. "I guess it was sad to watch," he admitted, "but those girls'll be all right when they get to their new homes."

"Would you?" Joseph asked.

Zachary squirmed uncomfortably. "They're used to it."

Joseph's mind whirled in confusion. How could everyone he knew be wrong? Zachary, his own father, the preacher, even his gentle mother believed that slavery was all right. Just about the only person who didn't approve happened to be the one person he didn't like.

"I have to admit that stepdaddy of yours is really something," Zachary said. "I don't know if that man is foolish or brave, but he sure isn't afraid to say what he thinks."

Joseph didn't answer. He thought about the way Mr. Byers had stood so fearlessly in front of the angry crowd. He had to admit Mr. Byers was very brave. Still, one man wasn't going to change anything. All his stepfather was doing was turning everyone in town against his whole family.

"I've got to get home," Zachary said, with a glance at the courthouse clock.

Joseph watched his friend until he turned the corner, heading for the mill. Then he hurried to finish the errands for his mother.

Clay was already home when he arrived. He was talking excitedly with his mother about his visit with Dr. Mercer. "I'll have my own room in the attic," he said. "And Dr. Mercer will let me go with him when he visits the sick. Of course at first I'll only be able to stand and watch," he added.

Mrs. Byers smiled at Joseph. "Dinner will be a little late," she said. "Mr. Byers isn't home yet."

Before Joseph could decide if he should tell what he'd seen, Mr. Byers walked in. There was a small bruise under his eye.

"We don't need to worry about those slave catchers we saw yesterday," Mr. Byers said. "Sheriff Underwood tells me their names are Bales and Scroggins. They're a pretty disreputable sort, but they left town this morning. Seems they found the runaway sleeping under a railway bridge."

Joseph started to ask what would happen when the slave was returned. Then he decided he really didn't want to know and pushed the thought out of his mind. The slave shouldn't have run away, he told himself.

Mr. Byers did not mention the confrontation on the courthouse lawn. He was quiet during dinner and afterward went straight to his desk to work on accounts. Joseph read a story to Jared while their mother did some mending, and Clay studied for his Latin examination. It was an evening like any other. Outside, a cold wind was blowing, reminding them that winter was not yet over. Tomorrow would be a Sunday, like any other, and then Monday Joseph would have to return to school. Nothing in his world had changed, yet somehow nothing seemed quite the same.

SEVEN

Trouble at School

Jared was just getting up as Joseph put on his coat. "I wish I could go to school like you."

"It's not much fun," Joseph answered. "If you don't know your lessons, the teacher makes you sit on a stool in the front of the room and everyone makes fun of you."

"Do you ever have to do that?" Jared asked.

Joseph shook his head. "Not yet. But I might if my penmanship doesn't improve. You just be glad Mama teaches you."

The weather was bitingly cold. Joseph tucked

his nose into his coat, trying to stay warm. He looked for his new friend, but Zachary was absent again.

Miss Graham rang the bell just as he arrived and everyone filed in. "Good morning, students," she said, as she did every morning.

"Good morning, Miss Graham," came the echoing chorus.

Elias Hawkins brought in a big load of extra wood to feed the fire. He dropped it into a wooden box near the stove with a clatter. Miss Graham looked unhappy. She tapped her ruler on the desk.

"Elias, that's supposed to be done before school starts," she said sharply.

Elias ducked his head. "Sorry, ma'am," he said. He scurried to his seat.

The school board paid Elias twenty dollars a year to sweep out the school every day and start the fire on wintry mornings, Joseph thought twenty dollars sounded like a princely sum, but he knew Elias gave it all to his mother. Since Elias's father died of cholera the year before, his mother supported them by working in Mr. Lippit's bookstore. An unwanted thought came to Joseph's mind. If not for Mr. Byers, he would be no better off than Elias.

"I'll give you five minutes to study for your spelling test," announced Miss Graham. "I want absolute silence."

Miss Graham sat at her desk grading papers. Joseph took out his book and stared at the list. Whomp! Something hit the back of his neck "Ouch!" he yelled, jumping up, nearly knocking over the bench and forgetting Miss Graham's order for silence.

Miss Graham stood. "Explain yourself, young man. Why are you disturbing my class?"

"I'm sorry, Miss Graham," Joseph said, trying to sound sincere. "I got a sudden cramp in my hand. It hurt something awful."

Miss Graham's eyes narrowed. "Hold out your hands, Joseph," she said.

Reluctantly Joseph did as he was told. He squeezed his eyes shut and waited. Miss Graham smacked her pointer stick two times across his out-stretched hands. "Now that," she said, "no doubt did hurt something awful." Without another word she returned to the corner.

There was a snicker from the back of the room, and another spitball hit Joseph in the head. Andrew laughed out loud.

Miss Graham turned. "One more laugh, and you will receive the same punishment, young man," she said.

Andrew's head bent down over his practice slate. Satisfied, Miss Graham returned to her papers.

Joseph pretended to study his spelling, but his eyes scanned the room. Everyone seemed hard at work, but Joseph spied the top of a peashooter in the pocket of a boy named Ethan. Ethan looked up from his book and stared at him. He patted the peashooter, taunting Joseph.

Across the room David Baker, the Quaker boy, gave him a sympathetic look. Joseph knew some of the boys picked on David because of his strange speech and wide-brimmed hat. He had noticed that David never fought back.

Joseph looked at his hands. The ruler had made a wide red streak across them. He was so angry over the injustice he could hardly concentrate. Even the girls seemed to be against him. From across the room one of them held up her slate.

"Yankee Spy" was written in big letters. When he scowled, several other girls giggled. They received a sharp look from Miss Graham.

It seemed that Joseph was going to pay for his stepfather's views whether he agreed with them or not. The morning continued in the same manner. Every time Miss Graham looked away, a spitball hit Joseph. At lunchtime everyone tumbled out into the small play yard at the back of the school. Joseph took his bucket and slipped out the front door, hoping to avoid his tormentors.

The school sat on a small hill not far from the business section of town. The stone steps were cold, but Joseph sat down on the top stair and opened his lunch.

This time of day traffic on the main street was heavy. Women shopped in the busy row of stores there. Their skirts were so wide that a gentleman walking from the other direction had to tip his hat and step out into the street to let them pass. Several large wagons rumbled by, heading for the train yard. Joseph heard the mournful whistle as the noon train prepared to leave the station. He loved to watch the trains as they chugged into town and stopped for passengers and mail and goods being shipped to other cities. Some people complained that trains were noisy and dirty, and it was true. But he loved them just the same. He thought his stepfather might feel that way too, although they had never talked enough for him to find out. He did know that Mr. Byers had been one of the people who had fought to bring the trains through the town. Everyone had respected his opinion in those days, before he'd decided to be an abolitionist.

Before the trains everything had been shipped by canals to the Ohio River, where it could be loaded on large barges and ships. But shipping by canal was slow. Now most had been allowed to fall into disrepair and dry up. Miss Graham had told the class that the towns still depending on the canals were dying. Even the people who hadn't wanted the railroad now admitted it was a good thing.

Joseph nibbled on his lunch of bread, cheese, and a piece of cold pork left from dinner the night before. He could see his stepfather's sash and door factory from where he sat. Usually it was a busy place, with wagons being unloaded or finished orders being readied for delivery. This morning, however, it seemed quiet. Mr. Byers's unpopular views certainly seemed to be affecting his business.

"Are thou all right, Joseph?" David Baker asked, coming out the door and sitting beside him. David was a plump boy who smiled a lot.

Joseph shrugged glumly.

"If it is any comfort to thee, my family does not approve of slavery," David said. "Nor the states leaving the Union. And there are others in town who agree."

"There are a lot more who don't agree," Joseph said bitterly. "Including myself."

David's face held a look of guarded disapproval that made Joseph flush red with sudden shame. But the look disappeared in an instant, and there was only David's usual round, friendly face. "Then it is indeed unfair for thee to suffer for views thou do not hold true," he said in his quaint speech. He quickly turned the subject to more pleasant things, and in a few minutes the boys were talking like old friends.

Joseph was surprised at how much he liked David. He too was fond of trains and admitted with a shy grin that he was often in trouble for running off to explore along the river instead of doing chores. By the time Miss Graham rang the bell signaling the end of lunch, Joseph felt as if he had made a new friend.

Several of the other boys glared at David as they walked in together. "Why don't you two move up north with the rest of your Yankee friends?" Ethan sneered.

Joseph clenched his fists, but David calmly returned to his seat, ignoring the bully.

"It is time for history," Miss Graham said as soon as they had settled in their seats. "Ethan, please tell me all the presidents and the dates that they served the country."

Ethan stood up and took a deep breath. "George Washington," he began, "1789 to 1797."

"Continue," Miss Graham prompted.

"John Adams, 1797 to . . . to—" Ethan shook his head. "I don't remember the date."

Miss Graham pointed to the stool in front of the room. Ethan slowly shuffled there and put the tall, pointed hat on his head. "I did not learn my lessons" was written on the hat.

The class laughed, and Joseph almost felt sorry for Ethan. Miss Graham allowed the laughing for another few seconds, then silenced them with an icy stare. Next she called on David.

Joseph's new friend took a deep breath. "John Adams, 1797 to 1801. Thomas Jefferson, 1801 to 1809." One by one he named them, ending with "James Buchanan, 1857 to 1861."

Miss Graham nodded. "Excellent. I see you have been studying."

The afternoon dragged slowly by. With Ethan glumly perched on the stool in front of the class, Andrew and his friends had a new target to torment, even though Ethan was their friend. They seemed to forget Joseph.

At last the school day ended. Before the bell had finished ringing, Joseph was out the door and racing up the street to the mill. He had been so upset on Saturday that he had forgotten to tell Zachary about the cave.

In a few minutes he could see the big stone wheel slowly turning with the flow of water from the river. He found Zachary hard at work loading heavy sacks of flour on a wagon. He seemed surprised and pleased to see Joseph. Two slaves worked with him. Joseph had seen them before, but he had never bothered to talk with them. Zachary, however, joked and talked with them as they worked. Samuel and Jefferson, the slaves, responded to Zachary in an easy manner, although they never looked at him directly. They fell silent whenever Mr. Young was about. Jefferson limped awkwardly as he bent under the heavy load.

"Can you get away?" Joseph asked Zachary, explaining about the cave.

Zachary glanced at his father, standing in the doorway watching them. Mr. Young was a short, powerfully built man with a brutish face. Rumor was that he often beat his wife, when she was alive, and his children. Today, however, he seemed in a good mood. He agreed that Zachary could go after he'd finished loading the wagon.

Joseph grabbed up a sack to help but, to his embarrassment, found he could not lift it by himself. He marveled at the ease with which Zachary handled the heavy bags.

Jefferson grabbed the other end of Joseph's sack and they lifted it together in comfortable silence. "How did you hurt your foot?" Joseph asked.

"The massa chopped off my toes," he replied simply.

Joseph was so startled he dropped his end of the bag. "W-what did you say?" he stammered.

"I heard my mama was sick," Jefferson said. "She's on one of those big plantations 'bout ten miles from here. So one night I went to see her. When I got back, he cut off my toes. That way he figures I can work but I can't run off no more."

From the doorway of the mill Zachary's father watched them with small, hard eyes. Joseph picked up his end of the sack in silence. He looked at his friend. Did Zachary know what his father had done? He must, Joseph realized. Then he thought of the rumors about Mr. Young's cruelty to his family. Maybe if you were around someone like that, you got used to it. Maybe you would get so used to it that even chopping off someone's toes wouldn't seem so bad. Another thought crept into his mind, although he fought to push it away. Maybe people had gotten so used to slavery they had forgotten how bad it was.

EIGHT

The Cave

At last the wagon was loaded and they were free. Zachary found some rope and an old tin lantern in a small barn near the house. He grabbed two candles from a box near the lantern and tucked everything into a leather bag.

"Ready," he announced with a grin.

As the boys walked to the cave, Joseph told Zachary what had happened in school. Zachary scowled and made a fist. "We need to figure out a way to make them understand you are not like your stepdaddy."

"Did you see your pa cut off Jefferson's toes?" Joseph blurted out.

Zachary looked away. "I saw," he answered. He was silent for a minute, and then he sighed. "Pa wasn't like that when my mother was alive. She died when my little brother was born. Then the baby died too, and Pa started drinking.

They walked in silence until they passed by David's house and saw him sitting outside on his porch. With a sudden impulse Joseph said, "Let's ask David to come."

Zachary frowned. "Isn't he one of those abolitionists like your stepdaddy?"

"He is," Joseph admitted, "but he doesn't push his ideas on you."

Zachary suddenly grinned. "I reckon he's a misfit just like you and me. Might as well be three of us."

Leaning over the whitewashed fence, Joseph explained where they were headed.

"We'll need some food," David said instantly. "My mother's making cookies."

They followed David into his house. Mrs. Baker was a small, pretty woman. Her dress was plain dark wool, and she did not wear the wide hoops that Joseph's mother did. The house was furnished as simply as Mrs. Baker was dressed, but it felt warm and friendly, and there were good smells coming from the kitchen.

Mrs. Baker wrapped a stack of cinnamon-smelling cookies in a clean white napkin. "What are thou planning to do with thy friends?" she asked.

David hesitated. Joseph and Zachary had already sworn him to secrecy. "We are just going to explore by the river a little," he said. "I will be back in time to do my chores."

Mrs. Baker nodded. "See that thou remember," she said.

"Come on," Joseph urged his new friends once they were outside. They raced past the houses on River Street. David panted along behind them, and Zachary and Joseph slowed up a little to let him catch up. They crossed a field at the end of town and a patch of woods to a ridge over the river. The water flowed below them, sparkling in the afternoon sun. Joseph climbed down the steep bank, and the other two boys followed without hesitation.

"Do you see the cave?" Joseph demanded when they were halfway down.

David and Zachary were silent, their eyes searching the contours of the bluff. "I see nothing," David finally said.

Zachary frowned. "All I see is that pile of dead branches left from the flood."

Joseph grinned. "Good. If you don't see it when you're looking for it, no one will find it accidentally." He lifted the brush aside, revealing the opening. "You must swear not to tell anyone. It will be our secret."

Zachary nodded. "I swear."

"Quakers don't swear," David said gently. "I will give thee my promise, though."

Joseph nodded. "Good enough." He lit the candle and placed it inside the lantern. The light flickered through the designs punched into the tin.

Joseph squeezed through the narrow entrance. He heard the others' gasps of pleasure as the lantern illuminated the first room. They quickly followed him.

"We are like real explorers," Zachary said in a hushed voice. "Maybe we are the first people ever to step in here."

"There's more," Joseph said happily. He led the way to the tunnel he'd discovered on his first visit.

A huge boulder jutted out from one side of the wall, but there was enough room to squeeze by. He held the lantern high. "Here's another passage to explore," he said, taking a step forward. Instead of the cave floor his foot found only air. Too late he realized he was standing at the edge of a crevice the other side of which was just out of reach. His body teetered on the edge. Then two sets of friendly hands snatched him back, and they all three tumbled backward and landed in a heap. Joseph picked up a pebble and tossed it into the crevice. It was a long time before they heard it hit the bottom. Joseph sagged against the wall, shuddering to think what could have happened if David and Zachary not been there.

"I guess this is as far as we can go," Joseph said weakly.

Zachary held up the lantern, carefully examining the first room. Suddenly he climbed over a ridge of rocks and shoved the lantern inside an opening high on the wall. "Here's another tunnel," he said.

"Be careful," Joseph warned as Zachary climbed up and disappeared into the new passageway.

A second later he was back. "It's great. Come on."

Joseph and David scrambled up the ledge and followed Zachary. He led them to an even larger room than the first. Stalactites hanging from the roof of the cavern glimmered in the lantern light. A wide ledge ran along one wall, as if some long-ago giant had carved out a huge sofa.

David gasped. "It's wonderful."

A small spring trickled along the rocks at one side. There was an opening at one end of the room, and peering in, Joseph could see that the cave went on. Later they would explore that too, he decided. For now, however, this was enough.

"What are thou going to do with the cave?" David asked.

"We'll just keep it to ourselves and not tell anyone else," Joseph said.

"It will be hard to keep such a thing secret," David said.

"Not if we're careful," Zachary said.

They sat on the ledge for some time, making plans. At last David jumped up. "I have to get home and do my chores."

They climbed out of the room and crawled back through the opening tunnel, leaving the rope, lantern, and candles a safe way inside. When they were outside, Zachary and David helped Joseph carefully replace the brush.

"We could bring some crates and make a table and chairs," Zachary suggested.

It was getting dark. Promising to meet the next afternoon, the boys headed for their homes. Joseph walked with a light step. For the first time in weeks he felt happy.

Mr. Byers, however, was not happy. Waving his newspaper at his wife, he burst through the door a few minutes after Joseph. "Listen to this," he shouted. "You know that Lincoln is traveling by train to the capital for his inauguration. He was going to stop at more than forty towns along the way."

Joseph stopped to listen. His mother nodded. "I know all that, dear," she said.

"There are already rumors of a plot to kill him," Mr. Byers exclaimed. "The railroad sent an investigator named Allan Pinkerton to track them down. He convinced the president to take a different train to the capital. Now the newspapers are making fun of him. Look at this." NEW PRESIDENT SNEAKS INTO TOWN LIKE A THIEF IN THE NIGHT, the headline screamed in big letters.

"It seems rather cruel to make fun of him," said Mrs. Byers. "All he did was take another train."

Mr. Byers seemed to calm down. "I thought you didn't like Mr. Lincoln."

"I can't help feeling sorry for him and his wife. Mrs. Coe just got back from a trip to the capital. She says it's an awful town. The streets are filled with garbage, and since it is built on a swamp, the flies and mosquitoes are awful. She says the White House is terribly rundown, but Congress won't authorize the money for repairs."

"Mr. Lincoln has worse troubles than a rundown house," said Mr. Byers. "He has the whole country to repair. The southern states are demanding that federal forts and supplies in their territory be handed over to them. Most of the federal troops are giving in to their demands. But sooner or later they will run into a commander who won't."

"Then what will happen?" Joseph asked, even though he knew the answer.

Mr. Byers looked grim. "The moment southern forces fire on a federal fort, Mr. Lincoln will have no choice but to declare war."

NINE

A Mysterious Visitor

Lincoln was inaugurated president on March 4, and the whole country seemed to hold its breath, waiting to see what would happen next. At home things were actually better.

In the weeks after their first visit, Joseph and his two friends thoroughly explored the cave. The first room they kept to store lanterns, ropes, and such, but they transformed the larger cavern into a comfortable room. A combination of crates and barrels was turned into a table and chairs, and a ring of rocks made a place for a small fire. They even had enough blankets and rugs to make a comfortable bed. The boys met there nearly every day, and a fast friendship had grown among them. Joseph was teaching his friends how to whittle, although Zachary's first efforts were so misshapen they all had to laugh.

"I can see it in my mind, but my fingers won't do what I want," Zachary complained.

David's attempts were better, but still not as good as Joseph's. Both boys enjoyed their new hobby, however, and many a pleasant afternoon was passed whittling and talking around a small fire in the pit.

Mr. Byers wore a worried frown most of the time. In addition to the business he had lost because of his outspoken objection to slavery, people were too concerned with the possibility of war to build or repair houses.

Clay had passed his Latin exam and was now living in Dr. Mercer's house, studying medicine. He came home to visit on the weekends, but only for a few hours. When he was home, he complained about Dr. Mercer. "He read a paper that said sickness might be caused by tiny creatures too small to see. Dr. Mercer thinks that if we use soap and water, we can wash these strange creatures away. He makes me scrub the examining room with strong soap after every patient. I wanted to study medicine, not be a washerwoman," Clay said.

"Dr. Mercer is a fine physician," Mr. Byers answered. "When cholera broke out a few years ago, hardly anyone in Branson Mills died. Other towns were not so fortunate."

Jared had been confined to bed nearly every day since the celebration. "Do you think that's what's wrong with Jared?" Joseph asked his stepfather one evening. "Does he have these tiny creatures in him?"

Mr. Byers shook his head no. "He was just born with a weak heart."

"What will happen to him? Will it get better?" Joseph asked.

"I don't know," Mr. Byers admitted. His face was sad. Joseph knew that Mr. Byers cared very much what happened to Jared. Even on the nights he returned home, tired and covered with wood dust, he still found time to visit Jared and read him a story.

Mr. Byers hesitated. "I've been meaning to speak to you about your friend Zachary."

Joseph bristled. "What about him?"

"His father has an unsavory reputation about town. I am not sure that it's wise to spend so much time with him."

"No one but David and him will talk to me because of you," Joseph said bitterly. "I like Zachary. He isn't like his father. If it weren't for him, I wouldn't even be alive."

Mr. Byers looked pained. "I didn't intend that you should suffer because of my views."

"I do," Joseph said steadily. "So does Mama. Most of the ladies at church won't even talk to her. But for me at least it's been all right. If the other boys had been friendly, I probably wouldn't be friends with Zachary, or David either," he added, realizing for the first time that it was true.

"I didn't know things were so difficult for you. I shall trust your judgment about your friends," Mr. Byers told him. He hesitated. "Perhaps someday you may even count me among them."

Joseph was so surprised by this remark that he couldn't answer. After a minute Mr. Byers turned back to his accounts.

The weather turned bitter cold and Joseph's breath froze in little puffs when he milked Daisy.

One cold dark morning, as he was milking, he heard a strange thump from the loft where the hay was stored. He paused, nervously scanning the dark corners of the carriage house barn. Then he heard a soft scrabbling sound. Heart pounding, Joseph jumped to his feet. "Is anyone there?" he called, wishing his voice didn't quaver so much.

"Meow," came the answer. Old Tom, a stray cat that lived in the barn and kept it free from mice, leaped down from the loft and rubbed against Joseph's leg.

"You scared me," Joseph said, sending a squirt of milk toward the cat. Old Tom caught it and drank. Then he licked his whiskers, purring his appreciation.

"Daisy didn't have much milk," Joseph announced when he brought in the bucket.

"Last night's milking was down too," his mother remarked.

Joseph nodded. Now that Clay was gone, he had to do morning and afternoon milking by himself.

"She'll probably be all right in a few days," he said.

Joseph had better things to do than worry about

Daisy. Zachary had discovered another tunnel in the cave, and today they were planning to explore it.

"Go then," his mother said with a smile, seeing his impatience. "I can't imagine what you boys find to explore."

Joseph tried not to look guilty. He had never told his mother about the cave. He put on a heavy coat and raced to the river.

Outside there was a light dusting of snow, and people walked hunched over, faces tucked into their coats as protection against the icy winds. Inside the cave, however, it was warmer. Joseph lit the candle in the lantern and put it on a ledge.

"What's this?" David said. He picked up a piece of paper that had been tucked underneath the lantern and read it out loud.

> *"I like your cave,*
> *It's very nice.*
> *I came before*
> *So this makes twice."*

Zachary groaned. "Someone else knows about the cave. That'll spoil everything."

"Who do thou think it might be?" David asked thoughtfully.

Joseph scratched his head. "I hope it's not Andrew or any of his friends."

David looked at the paper. "The writing is too neat to be his. I have seen Andrew's writing." He waved his arm. "Perhaps I should not speak so unkindly, but I doubt that Andrew is clever enough to make a rhyme."

They went through the list of boys they knew, but in the end they were just as puzzled as when they found the note.

The boys spent the afternoon exploring the new tunnel leading from the underground room. Unfortunately this one proved to be a dead end. They piled their lanterns and ropes in the first cave room, and Zachary led the way out.

"We'd better leave a note warning whoever it is about the crevice in the first tunnel," Joseph said.

"We don't have any paper or pencil," David pointed out.

Zachary tore off a strip of his shirt, and they fastened it with rocks across the tunnel. "Do you think they'll understand?" Joseph asked. He looked down in the crevice and shuddered, thinking of the terrible drop.

Zachary nodded. "It should make them stop long enough to see it."

They headed back to the opening, David in the lead. Suddenly he pulled back and flattened himself against the entrance. He pressed his finger on his lips, warning Joseph and Zachary to be quiet.

From outside the cave came the sound of men's voices.

Joseph stayed in the shadows, listening. "It's those two slave catchers, Bales and Scroggins," he whispered.

"What are they doing in town again?" David whispered back. "I thought they caught the runaway slave they were after."

The two men were walking along the bank, obviously believing they were alone. Hidden behind the pile of brush at the cave entrance, the boys could hear every word clearly.

"We'll search every house and barn in town," Scroggins was saying.

"That will take forever," Bales whined.

"Not if we get that sheriff to get some deputies and help us."

"Why would he do that?" Bales asked. "He doesn't like us much."

"The law is the law, and he's sworn to uphold it. He'll feel bound to do it."

Bales cackled. "We'll let the sheriff do all the work, and then, when they flush them out, we'll be there to grab them."

Scroggins snapped his fingers. "If that doesn't work, we'll bring in some good tracking dogs."

"He-he. What're we going to do with that five hundred dollars Mr. March promised us?" Bales asked as the two men moved out of hearing distance, heading back for the main part of town.

Scroggins laughed. Joseph could not hear the answer, but the wicked laugh lingered in Joseph's ears as the men disappeared from sight.

The boys scrambled out of the cave.

"What if they were the ones who discovered the tunnel?" Joseph asked.

"I don't think they would just leave a polite note and not steal everything," David answered, pointing to the ropes, lanterns, and candles.

"There must be some more escaped slaves around here somewhere," Joseph said.

"Do thou think we should tell the sheriff what we heard?" David asked as they walked home.

Zachary shrugged. "I think we ought to try to find the slaves before those men. Did you hear him? There's a five-hundred-dollar reward."

David looked shocked. "Would thou turn them in?"

Zachary nodded. "It's the law. We'd get five hundred dollars for obeying the law."

"I would help them escape," David said stoutly.

"Then you would be a fool. And you could go to jail," Zachary said.

The two boys glared at each other. "What would you do?" Zachary asked Joseph.

The question had been whirling about in his mind. "I don't know," he said finally.

The day that had been so exciting a few minutes before suddenly seemed less bright, and they walked the rest of the way in silence.

"You seem upset, Joseph," said Mrs. Byers when he arrived home. "Is something troubling you?"

Quickly he told her of the conversation he'd overheard.

"It is not our affair, Joseph. The law says the slaves must be returned. Even in his inaugural speech President Lincoln promised to uphold the Fugitive Slave Law."

"What if the law's wrong?" Joseph asked.

"Everyone believes that Mr. Lincoln will try to change the law. Until then I believe we have to obey it."

Joseph knew his mother was right, but he was still troubled. That the law could be used by people like Scroggins and Bales didn't seem right.

Jared was sitting near the stove playing with a small carved coach Joseph had made for him. "Are the horses done?" he asked wistfully.

Shamed, Joseph thought about how long he had been promising to finish them. "I'll carve them right now," he answered. He spread a cloth on the floor to catch any shavings and fetched the wood from his room. He had already whittled out the rough shapes. He was using a piece of weathered wood he'd found by the river.

Jared crowded close to watch. "They're going to be beautiful," he said, touching the smooth gray wood.

Mr. Byers arrived home earlier than usual. "No

business today," he told Mrs. Byers with a worried look. He took a moment to admire the carvings. "Have you done the evening milking?" he asked Joseph.

"No, sir," Joseph said, jumping up guiltily. Before he could reach for his coat, however, there was a loud, demanding knock at the front door. Mr. Byers opened it, and Bales and Scroggins pushed their way in, bringing a blast of icy wind with them. Jared leaned close to Joseph.

Scroggins had a red nose from the cold, and his hair had blown wildly in the wind so that it stuck out in strange directions. Flakes of snow glistened on his hair and scraggly beard. Bales was the quieter of the two, the kind of person you would never notice in a crowd.

"My name is Robert Scroggins," Scroggins said, "and this is my friend Cyrus Bales." His soft-spoken voice was in contrast with his wild appearance. "We talked before."

"I remember," Mr. Byers said coldly.

Scroggins smiled. "We know who you are too. Everyone in town has told us you are the man to see."

Noticing Mrs. Byers, Scroggins nodded politely. "Evening, Mrs. Byers. I was just about to ask your husband here what he knows about two escaped slaves."

"I know nothing about your escaped slaves," Mr. Byers said. "But if I did, I wouldn't tell the likes of you."

"I don't suppose you'd mind if we looked around," Scroggins said.

"I would," Mr. Byers replied. "As a matter of fact, I must ask you to leave. You're upsetting my family. I give you my word that there are no escaped slaves here."

For an instant Scroggins seemed to consider pushing his way past Mr. Byers. But something, possibly Mr. Byers's hard look, made him think better of it. "We will be back in the morning," he said, "and this time we will bring the sheriff."

Then, in another blast of cold air, they were gone.

Mrs. Byers sat down weakly in a chair. "What awful men!" She looked at her husband in alarm. "There isn't any truth to what they say, is there? You're not hiding escaped slaves?"

Mr. Byers shook his head no. "I haven't seen them."

Joseph slipped into his coat and took the bucket for the milking. It was cold, and he walked briskly to the carriage house. Daisy was inside waiting patiently. Out of the corner of his eye he saw movement, a whirl of calico skirts climbing the ladder to the loft.

"Hey!" he shouted.

A girl froze on the top step of the ladder. Slowly she turned, and Joseph saw that she was holding an old broken cup. It took him a second to realize the cup was full of milk. Daisy's milk.

"So that's why Daisy hasn't been giving enough milk," he said. "You've been stealing it."

"I'm s-sorry," the girl stammered. Her dark eyes were wide with fear. "We were just so hungry."

"We?" Joseph repeated stupidly. Then a second face appeared at the top of the stairs, and Joseph remembered where he'd seen them.

"You're the girls who were sold a couple of weeks ago," he said. Suddenly the whole truth dawned on him. "You're the escaped slaves?" he asked incredulously.

"Please," the first girl begged. "Our master bought us together. But then he sold my sister to his brother. They were going to take her away."

"Why did you come here?" Joseph asked.

"I heard what Mr. Byers said that day. So when we escaped, I pretended that I had a message for him. We asked people for directions to his house."

"So Mr. Byers knows you are here?"

The girl, Lily, Joseph remembered, shook her head. "After we came, I was afraid. I wasn't sure he would help us."

Joseph stared at them. When Zachary had asked him what he would do this afternoon, he never dreamed that he would find out so soon. The girls clung to each other, Lily looking defiant, Mariam afraid, waiting to see what he would do.

TEN

——◆——

The Escape

Joseph poured Daisy some grain and watched as she munched on it. His mind was spinning. If he did try to help them, he would be breaking the law. Besides, he didn't have a clue where to send them. There were stories of an Underground Railroad. Everyone knew this meant there were people who helped the slaves until they reached safety. But if there was such an organized effort, Joseph had no idea how to contact people who could help. The girls couldn't stay in the coach house; that much was clear. First thing in the morning Scroggins and Bales were sure to return. One thing he knew for sure: If he didn't help them, they would be sent back to whatever terrible punishment awaited them. He thought of the slave with his toes cut off so he couldn't run away again.

Suddenly he knew his stepfather and David were right. Joseph had loved his father, but in this his father had been wrong. He didn't know how he was going to do it, but somehow he had to help these girls.

"I'll do what I can for you," he said.

Lily's eyes narrowed, appraising him. "How can I trust you?"

Joseph shrugged. "I don't think you have any other choice."

His mother was just putting dinner on the table when he returned to the house. "I hope they find those slaves before morning," she said. "I don't want those awful men to come back."

Joseph was so nervous he could hardly eat. Several times his stepfather looked at him with a puzzled frown and Joseph forced himself to sit quietly until he could speak with his stepfather alone.

As soon as dinner was over, Joseph followed Mr.

Byers to the parlor. "What would you do if you knew where the slaves were?" Joseph blurted out. He spoke quietly so his mother couldn't hear.

His stepfather gave him a thoughtful look. "I would help them if I could." He paused. "Do you know something about this, Joseph?"

Joseph nodded. "I know where they're hiding." Quickly he told his stepfather the story.

Mr. Byers looked alarmed. "If they're in the carriage house, they're in grave danger," he said. "The sheriff will search in the morning, and they might even bring dogs."

Joseph jumped up. "Let's go take them somewhere else."

Mr. Byers grabbed his arm. "Wait. We must think of a safe place."

Joseph grinned. "I know where one is." He was so excited he forgot about the verse writer.

Even after Joseph had told him about the cave, his stepfather hesitated. "We need a plan." He looked out the window into the swirling darkness. "I don't see Scroggins and Bales out there, but since they believed we were hiding the girls, they may be watching. They would be expecting us to move them to another hiding place. We need a diversion," Mr. Byers said. "I could do something to make them follow me, and then you could leave in the other direction with the girls."

"How could we get them to follow you?" Joseph asked.

Mr. Byers frowned. "Doesn't your friend David's father have a wagon?"

Joseph nodded, understanding immediately. "I'm sure he'd let us use it."

"I'll go to the Bakers' house. I'll act suspicious, so if Scroggins has got people watching, they will follow. Give me a few minutes' head start, and then you lead the girls to the river."

Joseph nodded. From the kitchen they heard Mr. Byers softly humming as she mixed up dough and set it near the warm stove to rise.

Joseph and Mr. Byers exchanged a look. "There is no way we can do all this without her knowing," said Mr. Byers. "Still, the fewer people who know, the safer we will be."

Joseph thought. "I don't think she'll approve, but she'd never betray us."

Mrs. Byers listened with a shocked expression.

"We could be put in jail for helping them," she said.

Mr. Byers looked at her. "Would you have me turn them in?"

Joseph's mother hesitated only a second. Then she shook her head no. "Those poor girls must be starving." She went to the kitchen and began slicing meat and bread.

Mr. Byers bundled up in his coat. "Remember to wait a few minutes. And be careful."

Joseph nodded. "You be careful too."

Joseph watched as Mr. Byers slipped out of the house and walked quickly to the street. Then he hunched over and ducked behind trees in a furtive manner. The snow was falling in large flakes that made it difficult to be sure, but Joseph thought a man-size shadow detached itself from a tree and slipped after Mr. Byers.

Joseph put on his own coat. "Wait," said Mr. Byers. She ran upstairs. A minute later she was back with two coats, some mittens, and a blanket. She gave him a swift hug. "God be with you."

The snowflakes clung to Joseph's hair and eyebrows. He raced to the carriage house. Once inside he lit the lantern and held it high to illuminate the corners.

"Lily, Mariam, I have food," Joseph called softly.

There was a rustle of hay, and Lily's face appeared at the top of the ladder. Slowly the two girls climbed down the loft ladder and gratefully took the plate.

He stared at them in dismay while they eagerly stuffed their mouths full. Lily was younger than Clay, and Mariam was only nine or ten. Even if they made it over the Ohio River, they still had to cross the whole state of Ohio to get to Canada. How would two young girls survive the long journey to freedom?

Joseph explained about the cave. "It will be safe until we find a way to move you on."

He handed the girls the bundle his mother had sent. "Put these on," he said.

He waited while the girls buttoned on the warm coats and nodded. "We're ready," Lily said.

Joseph checked quickly outside. The sky was clear now, and there was enough moon to light the way. He took a deep breath and motioned for the girls to follow.

They walked quickly, Joseph first and the girls a few paces behind. House windows glowed with soft light, and on the next street a wagon rumbled. Most people were safe inside their houses, gathered around warm fireplaces and stoves. Joseph and the girls slipped from tree to tree along the road, heading for the cave. A buggy turned the corner, and they threw themselves on the ground until it passed. In the glow of a small lantern tied to the front of the carriage, Joseph could see two men deep in conversation. They did not even look in their direction. Still, he made the girls lie without moving until the *clop-clop* of the horses' hooves slowly faded out of hearing.

As they approached the river, a terrifying thought crossed Joseph's mind, and he froze. The dogs. They had forgotten about the dogs.

ELEVEN

———◆———

Hiding the Trail

Joseph's heart sank. If Scroggins and the sheriff brought tracking dogs in the morning, they would follow the girls straight to the cave. They might be able to avoid that by walking in the water, but it was freezing.

"Is something wrong?" Lily whispered from the darkness behind him.

Joseph quietly explained the problem.

"We'll make it," Lily said bravely.

"I have a better idea," Joseph said. He headed for the mill with the girls following, hoping he was right. It had occurred to him that they would have to trust Zachary with their plans. There was too much danger he would visit the cave by himself and discover the girls' hiding place. Zachary was a good friend. Even if he didn't agree, Joseph did not believe Zachary would betray his trust, not even for the reward money. There was a small boat at the mill. If they used it, they would completely confuse any dogs.

When they reached the mill, Joseph saw with dismay that it was dark. How would he explain calling so late at night? Zachary's house was at one side of the mill. To his relief he saw a soft glow of light coming from the windows. At least someone was still awake. He hoped it wasn't Zachary's father.

"Stay here," he whispered. Lily nodded and pointed to a small woods near the water where they could hide. Joseph passed the tumbledown shack where the two slaves lived. It was also dark and silent. Somewhere off in the distance a dog barked.

He reached his hand to the door to knock. Then, before his hand touched the door, it opened. A very surprised-looking Zachary stood there. His mouth dropped open. "What are you doing here?" he whispered as he stepped outside and closed the door behind him quietly.

Joseph motioned for him to follow. A safe distance from the house he stopped and gave a whispered explanation. "I know I can trust you," Joseph concluded.

"You can, mud boy. But tarnation! That reward money would've been nice." Even in the dark Joseph knew Zachary was grinning.

"We're in luck," Zachary added. "My father's asleep. If we're quiet, he'll never know we've gone."

"How did you happen to come outside?" Joseph asked. "Did you see me coming?"

"I was heading for the necessary," Zachary said.

Joseph could not stop the chuckle. "You'd better go. We'll be waiting." He pointed to the woods.

"We're here," Lily called softly when he reached the trees.

"Are you all right?" he whispered.

"I'm cold," Mariam whispered back.

"It's warmer in the cave," he said reassuringly. "We'll be there before you know it."

A twig snapped nearby, and Joseph froze. "It's me," Zachary whispered.

Shaking with relief, Joseph followed Zachary to the boat. Silently the girls climbed in, and Joseph after them. Zachary gave the boat a shove and leaped in as it floated free. A second later they were gliding down the river toward the cave.

"You thank your mama for these coats and the food," Lily whispered.

Suddenly Zachary rowed the little boat to the opposite shore. Joseph's heart pounded. Had he been wrong to trust his friend? "I have an idea," Zachary explained. "Go ashore here and run a ways. Then double back. They'll probably take the dogs across the water. If they pick up the trail, we can throw them off completely."

Joseph nodded gratefully. While Zachary waited, they climbed out and ran across a rolling meadow until they came to a fence marking a farm field. Then they retraced their steps. While Zachary held the boat steady, they scrambled back in.

"That was a great idea," Joseph said as Zachary pushed the little boat off and guided it toward the cave.

"I just hope it works," Zachary said grimly. When he reached the cave, he pushed the boat into the shore and tied it to a rock. They sat without moving, listening to the night sounds. They heard only the gentle slap of water along the shore and the rustle of dry leaves on the trees.

Joseph pointed to the cave opening. Their eyes had adjusted to the dark enough to see the dark smudge of branches piled over it. Quickly they climbed up the bank, and Joseph removed enough branches to allow them to enter.

As soon as they were inside, Joseph lit both of the lanterns they kept by the entrance. He handed one to Lily.

Zachary showed the girls the hidden passage to the second chamber. "You can use that lantern," he said. "No one can see the light from outside."

"There is a big crevice in the other tunnel," Joseph warned. "Better just stay in here. It's safer."

Mariam pressed against her sister, her eyes wide.

"It will be fun," Zachary said kindly, seeing her fear. "See, it's like a little house in here."

"We have to get back," Joseph said. "You'll be all right here until we can find a way to get you started on your journey. Don't worry. My step-father will find out how to do it."

When they climbed out of the second chamber, Zachary saw a small piece of paper they hadn't noticed before.

> *Thank you for the warning.*
> *It would have been a nasty fall.*
> *I hope my little visits*
> *Don't bother you at all.*

"What if this person comes and sees Lily and Mariam?" Joseph whispered.

Zachary looked grim. "We'll have to hope Lily and Mariam are gone before he comes back." He paused thoughtfully. "The notes are always in the first cavern. Maybe he doesn't even know about the second room where the girls are."

Once they were outside, the boys carefully covered the cave entrance. "I'll take the boat back," Zachary said. "You'd better get home in case they figure out the wagon was a trick."

Joseph nodded. "Thanks for helping me."

Using the oar, Zachary pushed off in the boat. "I

knew I was getting myself in trouble being friends
with a bunch of abolitionists."

"I'm not—," Joseph started to protest. Then he
chuckled. "I guess I am." He climbed up the bank
and turned back to the water to wave, but Zachary
was already out of sight.

Joseph raced home, arriving only a few minutes
before his stepfather. Mr. Byers insisted that Joseph
tell his story first, interrupting several times with
praise. "Good thinking!" Mrs. Byers clapped with
delight when Joseph explained about the false trail.

When Joseph finished, Mr. Byers began his
account. "They fell for it, just like I thought. Mr.
Baker and I took his wagon to the factory and pretended we were loading some new doors with the
furniture. Sure enough, pretty soon Scroggins and
Bales showed up with the sheriff. Sheriff Underwood wasn't very happy at being dragged out of
his warm house. They took everything off the
wagon. Then they poked around, looking for a
false bottom. And then they searched every inch
of the factory." Mr. Byers chuckled. "When they
were done, the sheriff made them load everything
back on the wagon."

Joseph was exhausted from his adventure. Mrs.

Byers insisted he go straight to bed. Even so, it seemed as if he had just barely closed his eyes when it was morning and he was awakened by hounds baying in excitement. He looked out his window to see Scroggins, Bales, and the sheriff coming out of the carriage house. A fourth man was holding the leashes of three brown-and-white tracking dogs that were eagerly straining to be set free. Scroggins was scowling more than usual as he pounded on the door.

Mr. Byers opened it only a crack, but just as he had the night before, Scroggins pushed his way in. He was followed by Bales and a grim-looking Sheriff Underwood. From outside they could hear the still-excited dogs.

"Those slaves have been in your carriage house," Scroggins growled. "Don't try to deny it. The dogs followed them straight here."

Mr. Byers did a good job of pretending innocence. "So that's what happened to Daisy's milk," he exclaimed. "I was almost ready to sell her, she's been giving so little lately."

Scroggins gave Joseph a hard look. "I suppose you didn't know anything about it either."

Joseph shook his head. "I heard a noise one

morning, and it scared me, but I thought it was Old Tom." He widened his eyes. "You mean, those girls were there the whole time?"

"Old Tom is a barn cat," Mr. Byers explained at the sheriff's questioning look.

"They're lying," Scroggins snarled. He turned to the sheriff. "I'll bet they're part of that Underground Railroad."

Sheriff Underwood stepped in between them. "The barn is a good ways from the house. The slaves could have hidden there without anyone knowing."

"Wait a minute." Scroggins whirled and looked hard at Joseph. "You said, 'those girls,'" he said triumphantly. "How'd you know they're girls if you haven't seen them?"

Joseph felt the blood drain from his face, but Mr. Byers stepped forward. "I told him," he said.

"And I told Mr. Byers," said the sheriff. He pulled a piece of paper from his pocket. "I know you have a warrant authorizing you to bring back the girls, but Mr. March also posted a description on the courthouse." He read aloud: "'Wanted. Runaway slave girl known as Lily, about thirteen years of age, about five feet tall, slender. Also, her sister, known as Mariam, about ten years of age. Owner: Mr. Frederick March.' "

Sheriff Underwood looked at Scroggins. "You just make sure that if you capture the girls, you return them to Mr. March."

Scroggins looked flustered. "What do you mean by that?"

"I heard a nasty rumor that the last slave you caught wasn't returned to his master at all. I heard he was taken to Georgia and sold as a field hand. You made a bit more money that way, I'll wager."

"That's a lie," Scroggins said. "That slave escaped from me. He just up and disappeared."

The sheriff stared at Scroggins. After a minute Scroggins's gaze slid away. "The way you worry about those slaves," he muttered, "one would almost wonder if you were helping them. Either that or you're just too trusting. I suppose you believe the story about loading doors at night too."

Sheriff Underwood pushed his hat back on his head. "You saw there was nothing on that wagon but furniture."

"Don't you see?" Scroggins almost screeched

with anger. "That was to distract us while someone else helped them escape."

The sheriff shook his head in disgust. "Those slaves have probably already crossed the river into Ohio. I'm tired of you accusing the good people of my town. Now I'll go follow along with the dogs. If the trail is going the way I think, we'll lose it at the river. If you call me again, you'd better make sure you really have something."

The man holding the leashes stood outside, barely restraining the dogs. "Let's go," he called.

With a mumbled curse Scroggins backed out of the house. The family watched out the window as the group headed over the path Joseph and the girls had walked the night before.

Mrs. Byers insisted that Joseph attend school. Zachary was not there, and Joseph worried all day. But Zachary was waiting for them when David and Joseph left the building that afternoon.

"Those hound dogs followed the scent right to my pa's door. He was mighty unhappy to be accused of being an abolitionist. He even showed them how he cut off Jefferson's toes."

"What happened then?" David asked.

"They took the dogs across the river. Sure enough, they picked up the trail. But in about half a mile the trail just ended," Zachary reported gleefully.

"Did they find the boat?" Joseph asked.

"Funny thing about that boat," Zachary said with a wicked grin. "It sank. Dogs couldn't smell much under three feet of water."

"I'll take them some food tonight," David said, "in case Scroggins and Bales are watching Joseph's house."

It took three days, but finally the arrangements were made.

"You have to separate," Joseph told them, carrying a message from his father. "They're looking for two girls traveling together. A lady named Mrs. Brown will take Mariam all the way to Cleveland. She's going there to visit her sister, and she has papers to show Mariam is her personal maid."

Lily shook her head. "I promised we'd stay together."

"It's the only way," Joseph pleaded. "You've trusted us this far. Trust us a little more."

Lily sagged on the rocky ledge. She put her arms around Mariam. "I'll find you," she said fiercely.

Mariam's eyes were wide with fear the next morning, but she nervously followed Joseph. "You don't even have to hide," Joseph said. "Just remember that Mrs. Brown is your mistress."

The carriage was already waiting when they reached the meeting place. "Climb in quickly," said a muffled voice. The woman's face was hidden by her large hat. As soon as Mariam had, the driver cracked his whip, and the horses trotted smartly away. Mariam leaned out and waved as the carriage disappeared around a bend.

The next day Mr. Baker took Lily, hidden under a load of furniture. When he returned the next day, he reported that Lily had been safely passed into the hands of the Underground Railroad. It would reunite the girls in Cleveland.

"Who helped you make the arrangements?" Joseph asked his stepfather.

"It's better that you don't know," he answered. "On each step of the way only a few people know the route."

Joseph suspected that it was Sheriff Underwood himself who had helped, but he said nothing more.

The cave seemed empty. Joseph went the day after Lily left to make sure there was nothing that could be used as evidence. He saw two cloth napkins his mother had used to wrap food she had sent. He was picking them up when he spied a familiar-looking piece of paper. He snatched it up. Written in the familiar neat handwriting was:

> *That was a really good thing you did.*
> *You should feel really proud*
> *And if I knew you better*
> *I'd tell you that out loud.*

The hair on the back of his neck prickled. Who was this person, and why did he leave only unsigned notes? Was he watching everything Joseph did? Could he be watching right this minute?

Joseph worried about the note writer, but he also worried that Scroggins and Bales would return, gloating that they had caught the girls. The two men had disappeared the day after Lily and Mariam had been tracked to the river and had not been seen since. Mr. Byers told Joseph that the sheriff thought they had gone to Ohio to try to pick up the trail. As the days passed with no news, he began to feel hopeful that the girls had made it safely to Canada.

"I got a telegram from a friend today," Mr. Byers said at dinner one night. He smiled at Joseph.

"Who was it?" asked Joseph's mother.

"A lady named Mrs. Brown. She said everyone had a wonderful trip and arrived safely at their destination."

"We did it," Joseph said, gleefully forgetting he was at the table.

"What did we do?" asked Jared.

"We became a family," answered Mr. Byers.

TWELVE

———◆———

Standoff

It was finally spring. Trees were in blossom, and green leaves unfurled as the earth awoke. In spite of the talk of war, Joseph was in good spirits. Every chance they had, the boys went to the cave. The note writer continued to leave greetings, always neat, always in verse. Sometimes there was a gift: a shell from the river, a cookie, a new candle for the lantern. But of the note writer himself there was no sign. At school Joseph studied the faces of his classmates, looking for some clue. Their faces remained hard and unsmiling, and he decided it could not be one of them.

The three friends went to the cave as often as they could, hoping to catch the person. David brought several fishing poles, and they spent pleasant afternoons sitting on the riverbank in the sun. The next day a note informed them that the writer liked fishing too, and there was a can of fine fat worms.

Zachary was usually the noisiest and most adventuresome of the three boys. Lately, however, he had been distracted, as though something was bothering him, and several times David and Joseph noticed he was bruised.

When Joseph questioned him, he shrugged and smiled sadly. "Pa is drinking worse than ever. He wants me to drop out of school altogether. He thinks I have enough book learning already."

Joseph looked at Zachary in dismay. "What does he want you to do?" he asked.

"Work in the mill," Zachary said. He sat glumly for a few minutes. "I wish I could join the army."

At his friends' stricken look Zachary shrugged. "Don't worry. I tried. They said I was too young."

Joseph's good mood disappeared. He walked home still thinking about his friend.

Mrs. Byers was dressed for town. "I'm going shopping. Why don't you come and help carry packages?"

Joseph nodded. They walked the few blocks to town. The streets were crowded, and people seemed tense and anxious, as though they were waiting for something awful to happen. Several people gave Mrs. Byers and Joseph unfriendly stares as they walked about doing errands. Mrs. Byers purchased material for a new dress at the dry goods store. At the grocer's she selected a fresh chicken and four oranges. "Fresh all the way from the West Indies," the grocer said as he handed Joseph the fruit. "Better enjoy them while you can. If the Union puts up the blockade like they say, we won't be able to get goods like that." His shelves were nearly empty. "The captain of the Branson Mills militia took nearly everything for the men," he told Mrs. Byers. "He says I'll be paid by the new Confederate government," he added with a worried look. "Don't know what the townfolks will do if the army starts taking everything."

Mrs. Byers finished making her purchases and looked at Joseph, weighed down with all the packages. "Let's get a cup of hot chocolate," she said, "and then we'll head home."

They stopped at a small restaurant and ordered two steaming mugs of cocoa. Joseph gladly put the packages down while he sipped from his cup. Outside, a company of soldiers in Union blue marched past. Most of the townspeople stared at them with unsmiling faces as they disappeared around a corner.

Suddenly Joseph jumped up. "There's Clay." He had not seen his brother for several weeks. Dr. Mercer kept him so busy he had little time to visit.

Clay spotted them and waved back. He came into the restaurant and sat at the table with them. "I can't stay long," he said. "Dr. Mercer wants me to deliver all these powders before dark."

"I think you grow taller every time I see you," Mrs. Byers said, patting his hand.

Clay smiled. "Dr. Mercer says next time he takes an apprentice he's going to make sure he doesn't eat so much. I have to go," he said. "We're awfully busy. All these men are in town signing up for the army. Sometimes they get to drinking and fighting. Yesterday Dr. Mercer let me sew up a head wound all by myself. It was one brother fighting another over which side they were going to join."

"Which one did they pick?" Joseph asked.

"One joined the Union army and the other the Branson Mills militia. Not too many are joining the Union army. Most of them will probably be sent to Ohio. I heard that as soon as the Branson Mills militia has a full company—that's a hundred men," he explained to Joseph, "they are going to register in the Confederate Army of Northern Virginia." Clay stood up to leave. "Anything new at home?"

Joseph looked at his mother. She was smiling slightly at their shared secret. "Nothing much," Joseph said casually.

Clay nodded. "Guess I'm having all the excitement in the family." He kissed Mrs. Byers on the cheek. "I'm glad I'm not old enough to join the army. The Branson Mills guards have set up a camp outside town near the fairgrounds. It's a miserable place. The men are living in tents, and one of them told me they don't get enough to eat half the time. There are supposed to be supplies coming from

Richmond, but in the meantime they're stealing chickens from local farmers. Most don't even have uniforms, and the rest have blue ones like the Union's. How are they going to tell each other apart if they're fighting?"

"I still don't believe it will come to that," Mrs. Byers said.

A man and woman Joseph recognized from church entered the restaurant and sat at the table next to theirs. When Mrs. Byers greeted them, they stared through her and then turned away without speaking. Joseph's fists clenched at the unhappy look on his mother's face. She patted his arm. "It's all right, Joseph. Being right doesn't always make you popular."

They gathered their purchases and went back out onto the street. A crowd was gathering around a wagon that had stopped on the corner. The wagon was gaily decorated in red and green.

"A medicine man!" Joseph exclaimed. From time to time peddlers came to town selling tonics for various illnesses. Usually they provided entertainment. Mrs. Byers often allowed him to stay and watch, but today she hurried them past without stopping.

Mr. Byers looked tired when he returned home from work. "It's started," he said. "Confederate forces demanded that the garrison at Fort Sumter turn the fort over to them. The commander refused, and the Confederate army has set up cannon along the beach."

"Where's Fort Sumter?" Joseph asked.

"It's on a little island in the harbor at Charleston, South Carolina. The telegraph that came to the newspaper office says that it's pretty well fortified, but the guns on the beach are pounding it continuously. They won't be able to hold out for long."

"What will happen now?" Mrs. Byers asked anxiously.

Mr. Byers looked grim. "Remember this day—April twelfth. They're firing on a federal post. Mr. Lincoln will have to see it as an act of war."

The next day the news was even worse. The small garrison at Fort Sumter had surrendered. President Lincoln was asking for seventy-five thousand volunteers to join the Union army.

"Are you going to the cave?" Joseph asked David after school.

David shook his head. "My mother wants me to

go to Abernathy's drugstore for some headache powders," he said.

"I'll go with you," Joseph said.

David looked pleased. "Come on, then." They stopped first at David's house.

David's mother gave him a few coins to purchase the medicine. "Thou might get hungry on the way," said Mrs. Baker. She handed each of them a slice of warm gingerbread to eat.

The town was bustling with activity. Joseph had never seen so many strangers. The Union officers had taken over the hotel for their headquarters, and a United States flag rippled gently in front in the breeze. None of the Union soldiers seemed to be about, however, and the building was strangely quiet.

Somewhere in the distance Joseph heard men singing. As the sound grew nearer, he could make out the song. It was the new one titled "Dixie" that so many of the southern forces seemed to like. The voices were loud, and now they could hear the sound of marching boots as well. Nervously David pulled Joseph out of the street. They stood in the protection of Mr. Abernathy's doorway and watched to see what would happen next.

The Branson Mills militia rounded the corner. Their leader was a captain in a neat gray uniform. The men, numbering forty or fifty strong, Joseph guessed, were garbed in an interesting assortment of uniform pieces—some in gray pants, some in blue. Joseph saw a few gray tunics, some work shirts, and even a few red jackets. Only a few in the front had guns, but many of the others brandished sticks and even large stones. The townspeople scurried for cover as the soldiers marched directly to the flagpole in front of the hotel and stopped.

The captain stared at the door, as though expecting someone to challenge them, but from inside there was only silence. Then the captain raised his hand. "Take her down, boys," he shouted. Immediately two young men who looked as if they would be more comfortable being farmers than soldiers raced forward to rip down the flag.

Joseph swallowed hard. He was not sure why he felt so sad. The flag was only a piece of cloth, he tried to tell himself. Yet it was all he could do to keep from rushing out and begging the soldiers not to destroy it. He could see from David's pinched expression that he felt the same way.

A rock tumbled off the hotel roof, startling the two soldiers who had run forward. They looked up as suddenly the roof seemed to come alive with soldiers dressed in Union blue. Each one of them was armed with a long musket, and they were aiming right at the southern militia. From behind the eaves of the nearby buildings more soldiers were visible. "Stop right there," said the Union captain as he stepped out from his hiding place behind a huge stone chimney, "or you'll not live out this day."

THIRTEEN

—— • ——

And More Trouble

For a second everyone remained frozen in place, and the watching townspeople held their breath.

The Confederate captain finally lowered his arm. A small smile crossed his face. "They have us today, men," he said softly. "There'll be another time, another place."

He gave an order, and his troops turned and marched away, with surprising dignity for such a motley group. They did not sing as they retraced their steps around the corner and disappeared back in the direction of the fairgrounds.

A few of the townspeople booed openly, and others grumbled quietly. But the Union soldiers held their positions. One by one people drifted away, and at last the soldiers lowered their guns.

"Did thou see that?" David asked. His voice quivered with excitement. "We almost witnessed a battle."

"We'd better get your mother's medicine and head home," Joseph said.

David nodded. "It's a good thing the militia hasn't received any supplies. I wonder what would have happened if they'd all had guns."

Joseph did not answer. He had recognized half the faces on both sides. The men had been ready to kill one another over a flag. Yet these same men had been friends and neighbors just a few months before.

Mr. Abernathy had been watching from inside his store. He went back to the counter just as David and Joseph came in. There was only one other customer, and Joseph looked at him curiously. The man had his back turned to Joseph, and he could not see his face, but there was something familiar about him. "Sorry to keep you waiting," Mr.

Abernathy said to the customer. "Here's your bottle of laudanum."

The man snatched the bottle and threw a few coins down in the counter. "You sure this will put someone to sleep?" he asked.

Mr. Abernathy nodded. "I wouldn't take more than twenty-five drops," he said.

The man pushed his way past the boys without looking at them. Joseph gasped in surprise. It was Scroggins's partner, Bales. Surely there wasn't another escaped slave so soon. But what other business could have brought them back in town? And why was Bales purchasing something that would put you to sleep?

While David paid for his mother's headache powders, Joseph puzzled over the problem. When they left the store, Joseph still had not thought of a reason.

Zachary was waiting for them when they returned to David's house. He was sitting on the steps, munching one of Mrs. Baker's delicious cookies. While David delivered the medicine to his mother, Joseph told Zachary about their adventure in town.

Zachary was thoughtful when he heard the story. "There must be another escaped slave," he said.

"There wasn't anything posted on the courthouse wall except for Lily and Mariam," Joseph said. "That's where they always post the notices."

"I'm surprised they would come back at all. The sheriff wasn't very friendly," Zachary said. He snapped his fingers. "That's who's camping along the river not far from the cave. I saw their fire and some wagon tracks yesterday. That's why I came to David's house, to warn you that it wasn't safe to go to the cave right now."

David came out of his house carrying a plate with several cookies and sat beside them on the steps. He waved to a young black girl walking past with a large basket of clothes. "Hello, Hannah," he called.

The girl smiled. "I can't wave. My hands are full."

"Does thou need help?" David asked.

"No, it's not that heavy. I'm delivering clean clothes to Mrs. Simpson," Hannah replied.

"My mother has been teaching Hannah to read

since she's not allowed to attend our school," David said. "No one knows that. If people knew she could read, they would say she was too uppity even though she is free."

"She looks a lot like Lily," Zachary said.

Joseph nodded. Then he frowned. An idea was nagging at the back of his mind. Before he could put it into words, a wagon rumbled by. The driver cracked his whip, urging the horses on even though the wagon was already traveling dangerously fast.

Zachary stood up. "Say, wasn't that Bales?"

Suddenly Joseph's thought became clear. "Hannah! That's who Scroggins and Bales are after."

Zachary shook his head. "Can't be. Hannah is free."

Joseph quickly explained to his friends what Mr. Byers had said about some slave catchers kidnapping free black people. "It all makes sense. Scroggins and Bales have a paper saying they're authorized to bring back two slave girls. The description of Lily would fit Hannah just as well."

"But Mr. March would know she's not Lily," David exclaimed.

"Scroggins might figure that, since they didn't get the reward for Lily, he'll kidnap Hannah and take her South. If anyone questions him, he has the warrant to prove she's a slave!"

Joseph nodded. "That's what the laudanum is for. All they have to do is keep her groggy until they get out of town, where people know her."

"We'd better warn her when she comes back," David said.

They talked for a few more minutes, but at last David jumped up. "Where is she? She should have passed us by now, heading home with her empty basket."

Joseph gasped. "That wagon. That's why Bales was driving so fast. They already have her."

Without another word the boys raced down the street toward the river. When they reached the riverbank, they slowed down, keeping hidden behind the trees.

Unlike closer to town where the banks rose steeply above the river, the land here was almost flat. "This is near where I saw the camp," Zachary said.

Tall grass gave enough cover to hide them as

they slowly crept forward. Two horses hitched to a wagon munched the spring grass. The wagon was empty. Motioning for David and Joseph to wait, Zachary crawled forward through some tall weeds. A minute later he was back. "She's there, all right," he reported.

"Is she all right?" David asked anxiously.

"Her hands are tied, and it looks like Bales is trying to force her to drink some of the laudanum," Zachary answered.

"Did you see any sign of Scroggins?" Joseph whispered.

Zachary shook his head.

"What should we do?" David whispered. "I could stay here and watch in case they leave, while thou go for the sheriff."

"That sounds like a good plan, lads," said Scroggins as he stepped out from behind some brush behind them. "Too bad you won't be able to use it."

A silver-colored pistol dangled carelessly from the slave catcher's hand.

"What are you going to do?" Joseph asked defiantly.

Scroggins smiled unpleasantly. "I took a little walk last night and discovered something interesting. A nice cozy cave." Scroggins scratched at his beard. "It occurs to me that you might have solved my problem your very selves."

"W-what do you mean?" Joseph stammered.

"I'm thinking that some boys finding a cave like that would probably keep it a secret."

"Are thou going to kill us?" David asked.

Scroggins tried to look hurt. "Me? I'm no killer. Lucky for you." He leered at them. "No, I think we'll just tie you up and leave you in the cave. I figure people won't start searching until morning. Sooner or later someone will think to look along the river. Maybe they'll even find your little cave. But by that time we will be far away from here."

Waving his gun at them, Scroggins made them walk to the campsite. Bales jumped up and grabbed his own gun before he realized who it was. He looked at his partner in surprise. "What are they doing here?" he grumbled.

"Don't worry," Scroggins said. "These boys are a little curious, that's all. But I have a perfect cure for snoops."

Joseph looked at Hannah. Bales had evidently succeeded in forcing her to swallow some of the laudanum. Her frightened eyes rolled sleepily, and her head drooped.

Scroggins prodded her with his boot, but Hannah did not stir. "She's not going anywhere. Bring that rope and come with me," he said to Bales.

The brush had been removed from the cave entrance, and one of the lanterns was outside. Bales lit the candle and squeezed through the opening. Still brandishing the gun, he motioned to the boys to enter the tunnel. "Don't try anything funny," he growled. "I'm right behind you."

Joseph followed Bales into the first room. He stopped once and immediately felt the barrel of Scroggins's gun against his side. Bales picked up the rope the boys had used for exploring. He held up the lantern, illuminating the main tunnel.

"Too easy to find them in this first cavern," Scroggins told Bales. "Check how far back that tunnel goes."

Bales took a few steps toward it.

"Stop," Joseph yelled. "It's dangerous."

Bales sneered. "You have something back here

you don't want us to find?" He pulled the warning strip of cloth aside without a thought.

"No, there's a drop—" David did not have a chance to finish. There was a piercing scream from Bales and a second later a sickening thud as his body reached the bottom of the chasm.

Scroggins cursed. "We tried to tell him," David said with a shaking voice.

"Shut up," Scroggins growled. He set his lantern on the ledge. "You," he said, pointing to Zachary. "Sit on the ground. You sit with your back to him," he instructed Joseph. He pulled a knife out of his pocket.

Joseph squeezed his eyes shut. Was he going to kill them after all? But Scroggins used the knife to cut the rope into several pieces. He tossed some to David. "Tie their hands together," he said. And make it tight or I'll just toss you all down there with poor old Bales." He watched as David tied their hands in front of them and then their feet. Putting down his gun but keeping it within reach, Scroggins now lashed David's hands and feet. With the remaining length of rope he tied them together, wrapping it around the three of them over and over. When he finished, they could hardly move.

Scroggins picked up the lantern. Slowly and carefully he inched his way down the tunnel to the dropoff. He held the lantern, trying to see to the bottom. He picked up a few stones and tossed them, listening for the sound of them hitting bottom. Convinced that Bales could not have survived the fall, he sighed. "He was a good partner," he mumbled, more to himself than to the boys.

He came back and stood for a second staring at them. "I sure hope you boys ain't afeared of the dark," he said with a nasty grin. Taking the lantern, he disappeared outside. A minute later the boys heard him stuffing the brush back across the entrance, leaving the cave room in inky blackness in spite of the bright sunshine outside.

FOURTEEN

—◆—

Escape

The cave was silent except for the dripping of water over the limestone walls into the tiny underground stream.

"How long do you think it'll be before they miss us?" Joseph asked.

"Scroggins is right about that," David said. His voice sounded calm, but Joseph could feel his body tremble. "No one will look until tomorrow morning. It'll be too dark by the time they realize we're lost."

"We can't wait until morning. We have to get out of here," Joseph said.

"We'll never fit through the entrance tied together like this," Zachary said.

"Maybe if we can get to one of those jagged rocks at the end of the ledge, we can rub on the ropes until they break," Joseph suggested.

"Maybe." David sounded doubtful. "First we have to get over there."

Joseph thought of that day at the centennial celebration. It seemed so long ago now. "We have to work together," he said. "If we push against one another's backs for balance, maybe we can stand up."

"We can try," David said, still sounding doubtful.

"All right," Joseph said. "Bend your knees so your feet are on the ground. Then, when I say three, push as hard as you can against my back. I'll be doing the same.

"One, two, three," he counted.

Straining against one another, they rocked back and forth until they were standing. "It worked," Joseph crowed. "I wasn't sure we could do it."

David laughed. "Now thou tell me."

"We have to hop to those rocks," Joseph said. "Zachary, you hop forward, and David and I'll go backwards. We'll count together one, hop, one, hop."

Counting together, the boys started off. The third hop, however, sent them sprawling on the hard rocky cave floor. "I think I've scraped my knees," Zachary said. "It's not too bad. Are you two all right?"

Joseph had cracked his head painfully on the rocks. He felt a wet trickle of blood on his face, and it was a minute before he could speak.

"Thou are hurt!" David exclaimed. "Is it bad?"

"I'm all right," Joseph managed to answer at last. However, when he moved his feet, he discovered that he'd also wrenched his ankle. He pushed against David, trying not to put weight on the tender foot. This time it took them several tries to stand up.

"Instead of hopping, let's just slide our feet along," Zachary suggested. They crossed the cave with a kind of walking shuffle. It was painful and slow, but they reached the rocks without falling again.

Joseph rubbed his shoulder along the rocks, eventually finding a rough place. "We'll have to move up and down against the edge of these rocks," he said. He did not tell his friends that his head hurt terribly when he moved it.

Zachary grunted. "I think it's going to take a long time."

"It's better than just sitting here, waiting to be rescued," Joseph said. "Every minute we wait means Hannah is farther away."

Thinking of Hannah filled them with renewed energy. They dipped up and down, up and down, pushing hard against the ropes that bound them together. After a few minutes David called a halt.

"We're going to wear ourselves out. I think we must just do a slow, steady pace."

Joseph panted. His aching head was making his stomach queasy. "Do you think it's working?"

"There's no way to tell in this darkness. For all we know, we could be halfway through the rope," answered Zachary.

They rested a moment and started again, up and down, up and down, this time with a slow, steady rhythm.

After what seemed like a long time, they stopped again to rest. "How long do thou think we have been here?" David asked.

"Hours," Joseph answered. He tried to stretch his tired muscles. "I wish we could sit down for a few minutes," he said weakly.

"It's too hard to get up again," Zachary said.

"How is thy foot?" David asked.

"Throbbing," Joseph admitted. "It's so swollen the rope feels like it's cutting into it."

"Then we'd better hurry," Zachary said. He attacked the rope with renewed vigor. They rubbed, then rested for a few minutes, then rubbed again. At last, with a final snap, several loops of the rope broke. Yelling in glee, they wiggled clear of the remaining strands.

Even though his hands were still tied together, Joseph was able to reach the knot tying his feet and legs. Scroggins had not expected them to get loose and had not noticed David's carelessly tied knots. It took only a few minutes to free their feet.

"I think we can get out of here with our hands tied," Zachary said.

Joseph agreed. Limping painfully, they inched along the wall until they reached the entrance. Zachary went first and pushed the brush free, allowing them to escape at last.

It was dark, but light from a full moon enabled them to see. Joseph sagged against the riverbank, feeling suddenly shaky. His head was spinning.

David looked at Joseph and gasped. "Thou did not tell me how hard thou had hit your head." He tugged off Joseph's shoe and shook his head in dismay. "And thy poor foot. Why didn't thou tell me it was so bad?"

There was enough light to see that the ankle was swollen and purple. Joseph rubbed it gingerly. It felt hot. Zachary scrambled to his feet. "You stay here. I'll get help." He climbed over the bank and disappeared.

While they waited, David picked at the knots binding Joseph's hands. He talked as he worked, but his voice seemed to come from a distance. Joseph closed his eyes. When he heard horses and shouting, he tried to rouse himself, but the sudden movement brought a rush of blood to his head. He was aware of people climbing over the bank to help. He thought one was Mr. Byers. As if in a dream he watched his stepfather cut the remaining rope that bound his hands and pick him up as though he weighed no more than a baby. He rested his head against the safety of his stepfather's shoulder and allowed himself to drift away into a darkness that covered him like a blanket.

FIFTEEN

— • —

A Present

There was sunlight streaming through the windows when Joseph next opened his eyes. A stab of pain shot through his head, and he closed his eyes again, grateful for the return to darkness. He was aware of someone beside his bed.

"Hannah?" he whispered.

"Don't you worry about her, son," Sheriff Underwood answered. "I telegraphed every town between here and the river. We'll have her safe by this evening."

Joseph drifted back into a healing sleep. When he next awoke, Jared was there. He bounced on the bed, nearly landing on Joseph's swollen foot. Joseph touched his bandaged head. "Dr. Mercer sewed you up just like Mama does the mending," Jared said. "Clay helped him. You didn't even feel it, 'cause you were un-un..."

"Unconscious?" Joseph suggested.

"Yes," Jared said happily. "I was worried," he added with a frown.

"We were all worried," said Mrs. Byers, bustling in with a plateful of dinner on a tray. She plumped up the goosedown pillow for him to lean on.

Joseph sat up, suddenly feeling starved. "Dr. Mercer says you should stay in bed a few days," said his mother.

"Did they catch Scroggins?" Joseph asked.

Mrs. Byers nodded. "The militia is blowing up bridges all over the state to slow down any movement by the Yankees. It slowed down Scroggins too. The sheriff in the next county caught him. He made it only about thirty miles." She paused. "Hannah's fine. As a matter of fact, she's waiting to see you."

She opened the door, and Hannah stepped into the room. She was carrying a basket.

"You and David and Zachary saved me," she said simply. She held out the basket, which was bouncing about in an alarming way. "Your mother says you can keep it."

"What is it?" Joseph asked suspiciously.

"Look in the basket and see," said his mother with a chuckle.

Joseph lifted one side of the lid, and out popped a wiggling black-and-white ball of fur. "Oh!" Joseph squealed. Then "Oh!" again as a little pink tongue licked his face. "Is he really mine?" Joseph exclaimed in delight as he looked to Hannah and his mother.

Obviously happy that he liked her gift, Hannah clapped her hands. Jared was still sitting on the edge of the bed, watching with a delighted smile on his face. The puppy bounced over to him and wiggled up onto his lap.

There was a paper in the basket. Joseph was startled to see the same neat handwriting he'd seen so many times before.

> *I'm glad to finally meet you.*
> *You saved me, that is true.*
> *This puppy is a gift*
> *To say that I thank you.*

"It was you!" Joseph exclaimed. "Why didn't you tell us?"

"I thought you might be angry that I found your cave."

"You can come anytime you like," Joseph said. "I don't think Zachary and David will mind sharing it."

Jared was holding the puppy and crooning softly.

"Looks like I'm going to have to share this puppy," Joseph said cheerfully.

"I gave David a puppy too. But Zachary's father wouldn't let him have one. David said he would share his puppy with Zachary."

"Do you like the puppy?" asked Mrs. Byers.

"He's perfect," Joseph said. He looked at Hannah. "You didn't have to give me anything. I really didn't do anything except get myself captured."

"If you and David and Zachary hadn't come along, I might be in the South right now, being sold to be a slave." Hannah shuddered.

"Maybe someday soon there won't be any more slaves," Joseph said.

"My papa says if that day ever comes, it will be a long time. The South will fight long and hard not to change their way of life."

The puppy curled up beside Joseph and fell asleep. He stroked his soft fur. "I have to think of a good name for him."

Jared patted the puppy's head. "You could name him Softy," he suggested.

"He needs an important name. Something to help me remember today," Joseph said.

"You could call him Mr. Lincoln," Hannah suggested.

"That's it!" Joseph exclaimed. "I'll call him Abe."

"That's a fine name," Mrs. Byers said. "Now I think everyone needs to let Joseph rest."

Joseph groaned, but in truth he was tired. After everyone left, he curled on his side. Abe snuggled close to his heart, and Joseph watched him. He thought about what he would tell his stepfather when he arrived home that evening. The country might be on the verge of falling apart, but together the Byerses would be strong enough to face whatever the future brought.

The puppy was sleeping. Joseph watched him until his own eyes grew heavy. After a time he closed them, and together they slept away the afternoon.

More about *Joseph*

The Civil (for civilian) War was the worst tragedy in the history of the United States. Americans had fought the English, French, Mexicans, and Spanish. This time, however, they were fighting one another.

The Civil War was fought over two burning questions: whether or not people had the right to keep slaves and whether or not individual states had the right to leave the United States and form their own government. Most people in the North answered no to both questions. Abolitionists had done a good job helping ordinary citizens understand the evils of slavery, and they did not want the Union to come apart.

In the South many people, while admitting that slavery was not a good thing, nevertheless thought it was necessary to their way of life. They decided to secede from, or leave, the United States in order to live the way they wanted. The northern states were not prepared to let them go without a fight.

By May 1861 eleven southern states had formed the Confederated States of America with Jefferson Davis as their president.

For many, the Civil War started with a sense of excitement and even fun. Young men joined the army, expecting to have an adventure and be home again in a few months. What they got was four years of terrible war that killed more soldiers than were lost in the American Revolution, the War of 1812, the Spanish-American War, World War I, World War II, the Korean War, and the Vietnam War put together. Nearly every family lost a husband, a brother, a son, or a cousin. Men died in the fighting and they died from disease and hunger.

Although Kentucky managed to stay neutral—refusing to join either side in the conflict—the loyalties of its citizens were sharply divided. Fifty thousand Kentuckians joined the Union army, and about thirty-five thousand joined the Confederate troops.

Here are some interesting facts about Joseph's time:

Dr. Mercer believes that cleanliness in the sickroom will help his patients get better. Most doctors of that time would have disagreed with him. In fact, bathing too often was considered bad for you. Doctors went from patient to patient without washing their hands, spreading the diseases they were trying to cure. One of the most common treatments was "bleeding," or draining "bad" or diseased blood from the body. This was done by lancing, piercing the skin (probably using a dirty knife), or using leaches to suck out the bad blood. These procedures only weakened the patient and made it harder to recover.

When Joseph goes to Zachary's house, the boy is heading for the "necessary." Did you guess what that was? If you said outhouse, you were right! If you were lucky in those days, your school might have two "necessaries," one for girls and one for boys.

The vendor at the Branson Mills Centennial Celebration calls out, "Goober peas, fresh roasted goober peas." Did you guess that goober peas are peanuts?